Dead Heat with the Reaper

Copyright © 2015, William E. Wallace

Published by Mike Monson and Chris Rhatigan

Edited by Rob Pierce and Chris Rhatigan

Cover design by Eric Beetner

LEGACY

BY WILLIAM E. WALLACE

Frank Trask never guessed he had a drinking problem. "I drink; I get drunk; I pass out—no problem," he'd say when people asked him about the large amount of booze he consumed.

At least that was what he said until the Monday he passed out before he'd had his first drink. He walked out of his West Oakland hotel to buy a package of razor blades, turned right, and took four steps before everything went black.

He woke up in Highland, the hospital for indigents, illegals, and the uninsured run by Alameda County. He could tell it was the county pill mill because the staff had stenciled its name on everything to keep patients from walking out with it.

The news crawl on the idiot box hanging from the ceiling above his bed told him it was already Thursday. Trask groaned. He was supposed to spend Tuesday at Pete's, his local bar, celebrating his 67th birthday with the closest thing to a family he had, his three buddies from the old steel mill.

Instead he'd spent his birthday passed out in a no-hoper hospital with a bunch of losers who didn't know where their next meal—or anything else—was coming from.

He could have worked up a pretty good case of feeling sorry for himself if he'd had half a heat on, but ordering a drink in a county hospital was out of the question.

Now THAT, he thought, *is a drinking problem: not being able to get hold of booze when you really need it.*

A nurse who looked something like Dorothy, the big sardonic woman on "The Golden Girls," seemed surprised to find Trask awake.

"Well, welcome back," she said, reviewing the readings on the machine next to his bed. "You've been out quite a while. How do you feel?"

Trask eyed her. He'd never had much use for the medical profession. "I feel like home-made shit," he said.

"Ah!" she said, smiling. "A Village Fugs fan. Tuli Kupferberg rocks!"

Her name tag said "Kennedy" in white letters on black plastic. Trask thought of asking her whether she was single and would like a husband; he hadn't met a woman who'd heard of the Village Fugs or Kupferberg since 1967.

"What's wrong with me?" he asked. "Why am I in county?"

She gave him a long look. "I'd rather your doctor talked to you about that, Mr. Trask."

"So where is he, at the driving range or something? How many times a month does he drop by?"

She glanced at her watch and smiled. "You're in luck," she said. "*Her* tee-time isn't until five p.m. today, so *she* should be by in about ten minutes."

He thought about that. So his doc was a woman; he wondered if she knew about the Village Fugs, too.

The nurse finished recording information from the machine and took his temperature.

"Looks like you're semi-normal," she said. "That's a little like a miracle considering when you came in here, you were at death's door. Please listen to what the doctor tells you and follow her instructions. You may just live to see your next birthday."

Trask laughed bitterly. "I wish I had seen the last one. It's a hell of a thing to spend your birthday on your back in a hospital."

She put his chart back in the rack at the foot of the bed. "I can think of worse ways to spend it," she said as she started for the door.

"Yeah?" he said. "Like what?"

She turned and said, "You could have spent it on your back in the morgue."

She left, humming the Fugs' tune "Wet Dream."

***

He thought about the expression she had used: "death's door." He had probably heard that

7

phrase a million times but never really paid any attention. Apparently death lived in a house. He had always thought of the skinny old motherfucker just wandering around aimlessly with his scythe over his shoulder, harvesting souls willy-nilly, sort of like the homeless guy with the torn straw hat and shopping cart he saw going through garbage bins near his hotel.

His head was sore where he had banged it when he passed out. He could feel a bandage just over his left eye, and whatever was under it was tender when he touched it.

When the doctor showed up—three minutes early—Trask initially thought she was an orderly sent in to change the bedpans or something. First of all, she was young, maybe all of 28 years old; second, she was black. Trask had never seen a black doctor who was a woman before. They had all been men. And every African American doctor he had ever met seemed to be at least 55. He'd been under the impression medical schools wouldn't give a black doctor a degree until his hair was gray and he had a double chin.

"Mr. Trask?" the young woman asked as she studied the clipboard she'd pulled from the foot of the bed.

"Yeah." Trask looked at the three other beds in the ward, all empty. "Since I'm the only person here, that must be me."

"I'm Dr. Lois Johnson," the young woman said with a thin smile, holding out her hand.

Trask took it, wondering what year in medical school doctors learn the hand-shaking tradition. To Trask, it made seeing a sawbones a little bit like visiting a used car lot.

"You were brought in because you passed out on the street," Johnson said. "Have you ever blacked out like that before?"

Trask shook his head.

"Ever feel dizzy or disoriented?"

"Nope," he said, then corrected himself. "Yeah, actually, I do. Sometimes when I wake up at night I feel dizzy when I stand up. My heart seems to beat fast then, too."

"Do you have trouble sleeping?" Johnson asked, writing something on Trask's chart.

Trask nodded. "Only at night," he said. "Days I can nod off on the bus, or while I'm eating lunch. Night's a different deal. When it's dark out, I only wake up to pee. It seems to happen to a lot of us old farts."

Johnson made another note. "Do you have abdominal pain? Stomach aches?"

"Sometimes."

"How often?"

Trask considered the question. "Maybe three, four times a week. I think it's

9

indigestion. I take antacids for it."

"Do they help?"

He thought about it. "No. Not really. Eventually it just stops. Or else I stop noticing it."

"When was the last time you saw a doctor?"

Trask thought a moment.

He remembered the last time he'd talked to a doctor, but he didn't think that was the kind of conversation she meant.

***

It was in 2003. The line boss, Mike Conrad, had pulled him off the floor for a meeting in his little glass cubicle.

"Frank, we got a call a few minutes ago," he said.

"Yeah?"

The foreman nodded. "We're sending you home for the day. Actually, we're sending you home for as long as you need."

He handed Frank a piece of paper.

"What's this?"

"It's the address for the Permanente Hospital off MacArthur Boulevard near Mosswood Park," he said. "Have Mildred in the front office give you a twenty out of petty, okay? Take a cab, not a bus; you don't have time for a fucking bus."

"What am I going to Kaiser for? There's nothing wrong with me."

"It's your sister, man. She's in the hospital

there," Conrad said. "We think you should go see her right away."

Gladys, his older sister, was his only living relative. She was four years older than Frank, but her health was good. He couldn't recall the last time she was in bed with so much as a cold.

Frank stared at the paper dumbly. "What happened?"

"I don't know, man, but the people at Kaiser said she was in a bad way. They told us to have you hurry. You may not have much time."

Frank didn't even remember the trip to the hospital. His only clear recollection was sitting on a little bench outside the intensive care unit with Millie's doctor, a guy named Wagstaff. The doc told him Millie had stopped at a mom and pop over on Piedmont Avenue to buy a pack of cigarettes. She'd walked in the door while a pair of robbers was walking out.

The whole thing had been captured on video: one of the stickup men had a gun. Surprised by her sudden appearance, he pulled the trigger and the bullet hit her in the forehead. Wagstaff said she was in a coma.

"Is she going to be okay?" Frank asked, even though he was already pretty sure of the answer.

The doctor looked guilty as he shook his head. "We did what we could, but I'm afraid she isn't."

***

They made Frank put on one of those little masks to protect Gladys from his germs, not that it made much difference: the only reason she was breathing was because of some big ass machine they had her plugged into. Germs were the least of her worries.

He sat holding her hand for two and a half hours, but she never opened her eyes or said a word. He finally let go when they unplugged her and she immediately flat-lined.

***

The man who ran the mom and pop was a Korean fellow named Jeon. He apologized to Frank about Gladys, who worked at a dry cleaners down the block and was one of his regular customers. Jeon filled him in on the details of what had happened.

The two goons who killed Gladys were Eddie Johnson and Raheem Ransom, two street guys who hung around the corner outside Jeon's store. The neighbors thought they were hop-heads, but Jeon said he'd never seen them using anything stronger than those 40-ounce bottles of malt liquor that members of the baggy pants brigade guzzle when they're standing on street corners pretending to be bad asses.

Eddie and Raheem ran after the shooting and the cops were still looking for them. Mr. Jeon didn't know where they might have gone, but he was an old-school gentleman: the cops had taken his security camera DVD of the stick-up with them, but the hard disk was untouched and Mr. Jeon let Frank watch it so he could get a good look at the thieves.

"These two are locals?" Frank asked Jeon when he'd finished reviewing the video.

"Yes," Jeon said. "They live in big apartment up on Webster Street, top of hill. Drink at Egbert's."

Frank nodded. Egbert Sousé's was a popular bar on MacArthur and Piedmont, only a few blocks from Jeon's convenience store.

Trask had never been the kind of man who sat around moping about bad luck. He liked to take action, even though he sometimes decided what to do while he was in the middle of doing it. That made for poor planning—or no planning at all. This was one of those times when planning was strictly an afterthought.

Frank figured the apartment would be crawling with homicide detectives, so Egbert's would be the best place to look for the men who had killed his sister.

He took the 57 bus back to San Pablo to pick something up at his apartment, then returned to Broadway and walked around the corner to Kaiser. He sat outside the hospital until the sun set, strolled to Egbert's, ordered a pint of Bud and a shot of Jim Beam Rye, and sat at the end of the bar that was nearest to the window. He pretended to watch the TV hanging over the back bar while he kept an eye peeled for Eddie and Raheem.

The only person in the bar when he got there was the bartender, a big blond woman with a Scandinavian accent. He had just ordered his second beer when the guys he was looking for walked in.

The bartender wiped a spot on the plank about two yards from Frank and put a couple of cocktail napkins down on the damp.

"What's it going to be, honey," she said, showing a dimple to the bigger of the two men, a fat dark-skinned guy in a stingy brim and a Raiders jacket whose pants were so loose his ass crack looked like it might swallow the bar stool he hung it over.

"Jack and Coke, Inga," he said, looking around the place casually.

"How about you, Eddie?" she asked the other man, a skinny fellow in a weather-beaten leather coat with a knit watch cap pulled down far enough to almost conceal the gold stud that peeked from his ear.

"Same, honey," he said, showing grille work that would have been at home in front of a 1963 Corvette.

Trask sized them up. The clothes they were

wearing were the ones they'd had on when they robbed Jeon's convenience store. Smart criminals would have changed outfits, but Frank could tell neither of these guys was bright enough to illuminate a pissant's parlor.

He slipped off his stool and picked up the narrow leather cylinder leaning against the wall behind him.

"I'll be right back, miss," he told the blonde as he made his way to the men's room, slinging the case over his shoulder.

The skinny guy in the watch cap flashed gold at him. "What, you going to shoot some pool in the shitter, old man?" he said, nudging his cruiserweight friend with an elbow.

Frank gave him a hint of a smile. "Nope."

"Then why you takin' your cue with you, man?" the fellow in the watch cap said, glaring at Frank with open hostility. "You think you leave it here us niggas gone steal the motherfucker?"

Frank gave him an even stare. "No—I'm not worried about you two chocolate drops," he said in a flat voice. Jerking his head toward the back of the bar, he added. "There's a couple tables back there. I might knock a few balls around when I finish taking a piss."

He turned and headed for the toilet without so much as a backward glance.

***

In the bathroom, he took a leak, washed his hands and dried them with the hot air blower on the wall, then opened the leather case and pulled out the thick end of his McDermott. It was appropriate: Gladys had given the cue to him on the birthday when he rolled the hard ten.

He'd been shooting a lot at Pete's at the time, using one of the bent sticks in the rack on the wall. She'd join him on Friday nights to sip a Bud while she watched him tear up some felt.

"Couldn't you shoot better if you had a good cue?" she asked one night when he narrowly missed sinking the eight.

"This piece of shit's all right," he'd answered. "It's a poor workman who blames his tools."

She hadn't said anything more, just handed him a heavy oblong box at Pete's when he showed up for his birthday get-together with his chums. He found the McDermott inside.

Gladys had spent more than 200 bucks on the damn thing, making it the most expensive present he'd ever received. But you could tell by her grin when Frank tore off the paper that she felt it was worth every penny.

Frank loved the cue; he was convinced it had improved his game from the moment he unwrapped it. Most importantly, it reminded him of Glad. As he looked at it in the John at Egbert's, a tear rolled down his cheek.

He thought about screwing the forearm to the shaft for a moment then abandoned the idea, dropping the skinny half back into the leather tube and hanging it over his shoulder. It would be easier to handle broken down. He hefted the cue in his hand. The solid maple felt sleek and heavy.

Clutching the heavy wooden rod close to his side so it was harder to see, he walked back out of the toilet.

The way he looked at it, the big guy—the one Jeon said was named Raheem—was the most dangerous. He was close to six-five and weighed 280 pounds, minimum. But the little guy was probably quicker and more likely to be carrying the gun they'd used on Gladys.

Frank knew that guns can give you a false sense of confidence and slow your reaction time. If you're caught by surprise, you can be packing heat and still be at a disadvantage against somebody who is ready, willing, and able to strike first.

Frank was that guy.

He walked back to the bar and used his cue like a whip to backhand the big fellow in the brim sharply on the ridge of his brow, the connection making a pulpy crack that sounded like someone splitting a melon with a hatchet.

The blow rolled the big man's eyes back up into his head and flipped him off the stool, his feet following him over in a nearly perfect backwards somersault.

"Hey, damn it!" the man in the leather coat said, his eyes wide with surprise, his mouth an "O" of shock.

Frank continued his swing with the end of the pool cue, crushing Eddie's right eye socket with the wooden rod. Blind but still dangerous, Eddie dragged a dark automatic out of the map pocket inside his coat. As he did, Frank jammed the end of the cue under his chin, burying the maple an inch deep in the soft tissue at the front of his throat.

Gagging and choking, the man in the watch cap dropped the gun with a clatter. He grabbed his neck with both hands, his eyes bulging as he struggled to breathe.

Frank raised the cue and swung it down on the crown of Eddie's head, driving him back against the plank. Then he did it again. By the third stroke, the blows were spraying the blond with blood across the bar-top, leaving a pool of red that drowned the cocktail napkins and the glasses of soda and whisky on top of them.

The blond cowered against the back bar, her hands alongside her face, squealing with terror. Frank picked up a cocktail napkin and wiped gore off the cue, then swung the case off his shoulder and dropped it inside. Panting with exhaustion, he squatted next to the big man and made sure he had no pulse. He didn't have to bother with Eddie: the man in the watch cap had slid down the front of the bar when Frank stopped hitting him. His body was still.

Standing, Frank thoroughly wiped the glasses he had been drinking from with another bar napkin, then turned and walked out of the place, leaving them on the counter.

As he left, he thought there was one good thing about ridding the world of a pair of shitbirds like Eddie and Raheem: nobody was going to spend much time looking for their killer.

***

"Mr. Trask?"

Frank snapped back to the present. He looked at Dr. Johnson. "What?"

"When was the last time you talked to a doctor?" she asked.

"I think about ten years ago," he answered finally. "Maybe a year before the steel mill closed."

The doctor stared at him. "You're a veteran, aren't you?"

"Yeah," Trask said. "Marine Corps. I got a round in the thigh at Khe Sanh in '68. They shipped me to the Army hospital in Japan to work on it, then to a Navy hospital in Hawaii. Took 'em nearly eight months to get me fixed up and by the time they did, my hitch was up and I mustered out." He grinned at the memory. "The docs said the bullet had missed my female artery by about an inch. I didn't even know I had a female artery."

"Femoral artery," Johnson said.

"What?"

"Your femoral artery, not female," Johnson repeated. "It's a major blood vessel in your leg. If you'd been shot there, you probably would have bled to death in a minute or so. You're a very lucky man, Mr. Trask."

Trask shrugged. "Yeah, that's what the docs at Camp Zama said," he replied. "But I ended up with one leg an inch shorter than the other, so maybe I wasn't that lucky after all. Could have saved a hell of a lot of money if I didn't have to get one leg of every pair of pants I ever bought altered. But I also limp when I walk, which gets me a partial disability from social security. So I guess there's an upside to every downside."

She heaved an impatient sigh. "Whatever," she said. "The point I'm trying to make is, you're a vet with a service-related health condition. Why aren't you getting treatment from the VA or from Medicare, for that matter?"

"I was on Kaiser 'til the mill closed in 2002," he said. "My doctor quit Kaiser about a year before to move to Montana. They sent me a letter to sign up with a new doc, but I never got around to it. Then the mill shut down and

I lost my medical."

"Look, Mr. Trask, I'm really not interested in the history of your HMO memberships. Why didn't you go to the VA when you lost your Kaiser coverage? Why didn't you sign up for Medicare when you became eligible two years ago?"

Trask frowned. He was beginning to wonder if this doctor was ever going to let him in on what had made him pass out on the street.

"I figured I would sign up for Medicare when I started drawing social security," he explained. "I just turned 67 so I was planning to sign up this week. As for the VA, I didn't go to them after the plant closed because I wasn't sick."

The doctor glanced up from Trask's chart. "Actually you were sick, Mr. Trask," she corrected him. "And you still are. You have an advanced case of cirrhosis. End-stage liver disease."

Trask laughed involuntarily. "Jesus, kid," he said with a nervous grin. "You must have aced the unit on bedside manner. You make it sound like I'm dying."

The young doctor didn't blink. "You are, Mr. Trask," she said, a trace of sadness in her voice.

***

"Sorry for being so blunt, but it is what it is," Dr. Johnson said. "When they brought you in, your skin and the whites of your eyes had a slightly yellow cast, a sign of jaundice caused by improper liver function. You also had extensive spider veining and puffy nipples, a condition called gynecomastia. Both can be associated with cirrhosis.

"So we ran a bunch of blood tests and a liver panel on you and the results were unmistakable: you had elevated AST and ALT and your bilirubin count was way up, 5-6 milligrams per deciliter. Your ALP levels were off the chart. All are symptoms of decreased liver function. We did an ultrasound and found enlargement of the spleen and shrinkage of the liver."

Trask had no idea what all the alphabet soup was about, but he understood cirrhosis and improper liver function. He knew what it meant when she said he was dying.

"Every test we ran, the results were worse," she said. "Your liver biopsy showed advanced hepatocellular carcinoma, a relatively rare type of cancer, at least in this country. It's invariably fatal. You've apparently had cirrhosis several years, probably before you lost your medical coverage. If you had seen your doctors at Kaiser more frequently, they might have been able to at least slow the deterioration of your liver. But that was then and this is now. As we sit here, your liver is practically gone."

For the first time in his life he could

remember, Trask was speechless. But it didn't take him long to recover. "Can you do anything for me?" he asked in a shaky voice.

The young doctor inhaled before shaking her head slowly. "For a severely damaged liver, the only realistic option is a transplant. But your cancer is too far advanced. To be brutally honest, when we got back all these results, we weren't surprised you'd passed out on the street. What we couldn't figure out was why you were still breathing."

"What kind of time do I have left?"

"I can't tell you," she said. "You're day-to-day. With end-stage liver disease, we use something called MELD to determine a patient's chances of surviving longer than 90 days. If I were a betting woman, I'd wager you don't make it that long."

Trask shook his head. "What a pisser," he said, his voice shaky. "Cirrhosis and liver cancer. And I don't even drink that much. I can only remember getting really shitfaced a few times in my life."

"How much alcohol do you usually consume?"

"I dunno," he said. "Maybe five, six drinks a night. That's over the course of four or five hours of socializing. A lot of times I don't even feel like I'm getting high."

"Even four drinks a day can be ruinous to your liver, Mr. Trask," she said, closing her eyes briefly to calculate. "Let me see: five or six drinks a day with an ounce of liquor in each one, seven days a week. That's between fourteen and seventeen gallons of alcohol a year."

"You missed your calling."

"What do you mean?"

"You're good enough with numbers to be an accountant," he said with an attempt at a smile. "But I get the point. I thought I was doing better than my old man who was a really heavy drinker, but I guess you don't have to drink a quart a day to kill yourself."

"What happened to your father?"

"He died of cirrhosis when I was 19."

"Well, there you go," she said. "You're too healthy to stay in the hospital, I'm afraid. The next time you have another attack like the one that put you in here it will probably be fatal. It could be weeks—maybe even months. I don't know."

Trask sagged back in the bed. It was a hell of a piece of news to get right after your 67th birthday.

"So, what do I do?" he asked.

The doctor's expression was sad and earnest. "There's no medication you can take for this. There's no cure. It would be stupid for us to even tell you to stop drinking, frankly. You're past the point of recovering or even substantially prolonging your life. The simple fact is, sooner or later, all of us die. For you, it's just going to be sooner." She locked eyes with him. "Mr. Trask—

Frank: I'll be really blunt," she said, so quietly Trask could hear a patient coughing in a ward down the hall. "If I were you, I'd get my affairs in order and take care of any business you need to handle before you die." She put her hand on his and gave it a pat. "I'd get the most out of every day you have left because the fact of the matter is, it could be your last."

***

Trask walked up Beaumont to MacArthur to catch the bus, then got off at 34th Street to hike back to the hotel where he lived. The bus was nearly empty and the trip took almost a half hour, plenty of time for him to think about the crab eating away inside him.

He was still shaken by the news. He'd thought of himself as an old bastard for years already, but he wasn't really. A magazine article he'd read in the barber shop a few months earlier said the average American man was a little over 77 when he croaked. He'd never make it that far, he thought.

Trask's old man had been 70 when he bought the farm. Frank had been just finishing up boot camp in San Diego at the time.

"We'll give you leave so you can go home for the funeral," his D.I. had told him.

"What for?" Frank asked.

"It's called bereavement leave, private. It's a

chance to take care of any personal business your old man left behind."

Frank shrugged. "He didn't leave any business that my older sister can't take care of," he said. "He's got a deal with some outfit to be cremated. She'll hold onto his ashes until I get out of the corps. And if I don't make it, she'll take care of them herself."

And that was that. His old man had died at 70 and Trask hadn't even gone to his funeral. It was almost certain Frank would die younger than his dad. Didn't seem fair, somehow. Wasn't each generation supposed to live a little longer than the last one?

He'd liked his father—he didn't throw the word "love" around lightly, but he had to admit he loved the old guy. Still, the thought that his old man had lived three more years than he would pissed him off a little.

He mulled over what Doctor Johnson had said about getting the most out of what time he had left.

Trask wasn't sure how to go about it. His life revolved around reading the morning paper, walking from the hotel to the corner store and bullshitting with a few old buddies who used to work at the plant.

He ate a soft-boiled egg and half a toasted English muffin every day and had canned soup or chili for dinner most nights. Sometimes he picked up a snack from the store, a mom and pop operation run by some Palestinian folks who always seemed glad to see him, probably because they knew he wouldn't try to light-finger their merchandise.

A few times a week he broke bread with one or two of his friends at the soul food joint next to Pete's Tavern. The bar was where he spent most of his time. Pete's was really the center of his social life and it had been for nearly 30 years.

It wasn't much of a life, really. He had no idea how to get the most out of it. It seemed to him he already was.

"If Glad was still alive, she'd be able to tell me what to do," he muttered to himself.

His sister was always the kid with more sense in the family. After Frank's old man croaked, Glad was the adult of the pair—the person he talked to when he had a big decision to make and didn't know what to do; the one he went to when he was having trouble of some sort. They weren't remotely alike, but they were close anyway.

***

The two knuckleheads that hung out on the corner were sitting on the stoop of the building next to the Carlson when Frank got off the bus.

"Hey, old timer," the one called Lenny shouted. "We missed you while you were gone.

You take a vacation or something?"

Frank didn't feel like talking about his impending doom. "Something," he shouted back. "I better not find out you two shitbirds caused any trouble while I was gone or I'll come back and kick your asses."

The two street guys laughed good naturedly. "You would, too, I bet," Lenny said. "Tell you what—you want to kick somebody's ass, pick on Bob here. I'll hold his coat."

They laughed again.

"Don't piss me off or you'll need somebody to hold both of your coats," Frank said gruffly, shooting a grin at the pair.

Not a pair of bad guys, really, he thought as he climbed the steps. *They just dress like they're heading out to rob a 7-Eleven. Actually, they're pretty nice people, all things considered.*

He entered the Carlson. As he did, he noticed his legs were a little shaky. He wondered if it was because of the cancer or just because the walk and bus trip had tired him after he'd spent a couple days on his back.

That was another thing that pissed him off: the thought that he would spend whatever time he had left worrying whether it was some kind of new symptom every time he sneezed or cut a fart.

"Jesus Christ, try to get a grip," he muttered to himself as he unlocked the door. "You start panicking every time your head aches or you get constipated, you really *will* make yourself sick."

Inside, the residence hotel was as gloomy as ever, lit only by sun through the windows that ran from entry to eaves. Trask sighed as he climbed to the third floor, taking it slowly and using the handrail on the wall. The banister was still loose on the landing outside his flat and it was a long way down to the tile floor at the bottom, so he moved to the other side out of caution.

I may be dying, but there's no reason to hurry things along.

As he was unlocking his door, Natalie Hatfield emerged from the next flat, her little shopping satchel on her arm and her six-month-old baby in a pack on her back. She gave Frank her usual shy, frightened smile and darted past, scared to talk with him because her psycho husband, Cliff, might hear about it and slap her around out of sheer jealousy. She had a shiner around her left eye turning greenish-brown as it faded.

"Watch the handrail, Natalie," he said. "It's about ready to collapse. Somebody's going to grab it someday and fall all the way down into the lobby. I'd hate for it to be you and Lucy."

"Thanks, Mr. Trask," she whispered as she rushed by. "I'll mention it to Mrs. Hung."

He watched her hurry down the stairs, knowing she wasn't going to say anything to the landlady; she wouldn't dare. He heard Cliff scream at her almost every night through the wall between their flats, calling her a slut and cunt, and warning her he'd kill her if she spoke to any of the people in the Carlson Inn, even Mrs. Hung. He backed up his threats by beating her for no good reason. Frank would bet his next retirement check her black eye was a present from Cliff.

Trask thought the fucker should be in jail; better yet, dead.

The half cup of coffee Frank had left on the counter next to the sink had grown a little green jungle of moldy stuff on its top during the time he was in the hospital. Reminded him of what Vietnam looked like from the helicopter taking him to Khe Sanh. He flushed the green stuff down the toilet and rinsed the cup in the sink before putting it aside to wash later.

Sitting down at the little built-in breakfast nook he took stock of what he called home: a toilet, kitchenette, and another room mostly filled with a twin bed. He had a little portable TV he rarely watched, a single melamine place setting, a toaster, fry pan, an aluminum pot with a plastic handle, and a mug and a filter top he used to brew coffee one cup at a time.

All the rest of the furniture came with the apartment: the bed, the little coffee table, the chest of drawers, the cook-top in the kitchenette and the refrigerator right next to it. His only clothes filled two of the four drawers in the dresser and a couple hangers in the tiny closet. His bathroom towels had come from St. Vincent DePaul.

Trask sighed. His life was simple, all right; if he'd gotten married and raised kids, there wouldn't be much for them to fight over when he croaked.

It's not much of a legacy. Good thing I saved my kids from disappointment by never having them in the first place.

The thought reminded Trask that he had no idea what kind of financial shape he was in. It had been years since he had actually looked at his statements from the credit union where his money was. When they came each month, he tossed the old one out and put the new one in the "go to hell" drawer in his dresser.

He went to the chest and slid the drawer open. Inside was his most recent Social Security statement, a pair of reading glasses with a missing lens, a couple of clean handkerchiefs he never used, and some correspondence from the bank in L.A. that sent him his retirement check each month.

He found his credit union statement at the bottom in a bundle of open envelopes with a rubber band around them. He'd never even opened the damned thing. He left the envelopes and band on his dresser and took

31

the statement back to the breakfast nook.

Frank was 58 when the steel mill had closed, so he got an early retirement from the union's Taft-Hartley trust, $2,100 a month. The check covered his rent and left him with $900 for any other expenses he might have. He rarely spent more than $800 a month on food, his bar bill, and incidentals, so over the last nine years he had managed to salt away nearly $11,000 in his savings account.

His leg qualified him for veteran's disability when he first got out of the service, but he got the job at the mill about a year after he started receiving VA checks. Although that should have ended his eligibility, for some reason, the $400-a-month checks had never stopped. Trask deposited the VA money into a separate savings account at the credit union. He'd figured someday the feds might realize their mistake and come knocking on his door. He wanted to be able to return all the cash if they did.

At the same time, he'd stuck $600 each month from his steel mill paychecks into a separate credit union account through an allotment. He'd left both accounts alone all these years, never even bothered to check the balances.

He opened the envelope with his credit union statement and pored over it until he found the bottom line for each account. The VA money totaled roughly $200,000 including interest; the payroll savings came to another $230,000.

He gave a low whistle. He had more than $400,000 to work with; if he'd had kids, maybe they wouldn't have been disappointed after all.

He put the bundle of envelopes away, hiding it down under the other junk as if it contained the actual cash. *Now is as good a day as any to use that money. The question is: what am I going to do with it?*

Gladys would know. Hell, if she were still here, I'd just leave it all to her in the first place.

He felt a pang of loneliness. He'd missed his sister since the day she died, but he'd never missed her as much as he did now.

***

"Hey, Frank," Sam Jorgensen said. "Where the hell you been? We had a little birthday party all put together for you, with cake and everything. Nobody could figure out where you were."

Jorgensen was at the back table in Pete's, the one under the sign "Geezers Only." With him were Ferdie Gonzales and Bill Habersham. The three old-timers had worked with Trask at the steel mill for at least 20 years and all three were also early retirees. Except for Joe Brundage, the bartender, they were the only people in the joint. That figured; it was just 3:30 p.m.

Trask stopped at the jukebox long enough to put in money and punch numbers from memory.

He pulled a chair over from one of the other tables and sat down with a grunt as John Fogerty began singing "Who'll Stop the Rain?"

"I took a header out front of the Carlson and ended up at Highland," he said, pointing to the bandage on his forehead before signaling Joe to bring a round for the table.

"Oh, man!" said Ferdie, who lived on the second floor. "Right in front of the hotel? I asked Mrs. Hung where you were and she said she didn't know. Didn't anybody see you fall?"

"Nope," Trask said. "The people at Highland told me a passing cab driver saw me go down and had his dispatcher call 9-1-1, then hung around until the paramedics got there and took me to county. It was probably around 9:30 in the morning. There's never anybody on the street that time of day."

"Yeah, the crackheads all sleep in until at least noon," Habersham said, finishing his beer as Brundage brought the fresh drinks.

"I couldn't help but overhear you, Frank," Joe said. "You okay? I see you got a wound on your gourd. You were gone for what? Like three-four days or something? You spend the whole time at the hospital?"

Trask nodded. "Yeah," he said. "They ran a bunch of tests on me and shit. I guess I was out for most of the time there. They kicked me out when I finally woke up."

"Did somebody whack you or something?" Habersham asked. Bill packed a gun most of the time. He thought everybody in West Oakland was a crook or worse. He lived in terror of being robbed by some junkie looking for drug money.

"Naw," Trask said as Brundage set a Seven and Seven in front of him. He could smell the whisky in the drink; Joe had a generous hand. "I was already out when I went down. They told me I got this ding when I banged my head on the way."

Jorgensen peered at him closely. "Why'd you conk out, Frank?"

Trask figured the best way to give them the bad news was just the way Johnson had given it to him: just put it out there straight, no chaser.

"The doc told me I got what they call end-stage liver cancer," he said, quietly. "Cirrhosis. My liver's the size of a peanut, all scar tissue and shit. That's what made me pass out. There's nothing they can do for me," he added, spreading his hands in a gesture of indifference. "My ticket could get punched just about any day."

For a minute, nobody spoke. Ferdie was the first to break the silence.

"Oh, man!" he said. "That's the shits, Frank. What you going to do?"

Trask gave him a slight smile. "I'm going to

fucking die, Ferd, that's what I'm going to do. I don't see any way to avoid it."

Brundage, still standing next to the table, looked at Trask's cocktail. Frank hadn't touched it yet. "Cirrhosis, huh?" he said. "Maybe you want me to take the booze away, then?"

Trask picked up the glass with a grin and took a sip. "Fuck, no. She told me it didn't make any difference if I stopped drinking now or not, I'm too far gone."

"She?" Jorgensen asked.

"My doctor. First woman doctor I ever had. Looks like she's gonna be the last, too."

"Women," Habersham said dismissively. He'd had a bad divorce ten years ago and was still dealing with the legal fallout. "What do they know?"

Trask laughed. "This one knows a hell of a lot more than any of the knuckleheads sitting at this table," he said. "She's young, but she didn't diddle me around. She said every test they gave me confirmed it: I'm dying. Could be days, could be as much as a month or two, but I'm going. She just told me straight, the way I did you. She's all right. Young, maybe, but she's okay."

There was another minute of uncomfortable silence.

"What a fucking bummer," Jorgensen said,

picking up his beer and draining a third of it in one long swallow.

Trask shrugged and had another taste of his drink. "We all gotta go sometime."

Jorgensen smiled at Frank's matter-of-fact attitude. "You always were a tough sonofabitch. I remember the time the I-bar they were moving with that winch came loose and broke your arm. You just told the line supervisor you needed medical and went to the lunchroom and sat down. You didn't even say ouch."

Trask rolled his eyes. "There's a difference between being tough and being in shock, Sam."

Jorgensen snorted. "Shock, my ass. The first thing you did was shut down the line and tell Livy to secure the loose beam. That's pretty clear thinking for a guy in shock."

Trask snorted with exasperation. It annoyed him to have people talk him up. Made him feel warm and fuzzy. He preferred things hard-edged.

"Yeah, well if I hadn't, the next person it hit might have caught it in the head," he said. "Then it would have been a workplace fatal instead of an injury. That means a shut-down while OSHA investigates. None of us could afford to have the mill sit idle."

Jorgensen swigged some beer, his smile lingering. "That's what I'm talking about," he said, shaking his head in disbelief. "Your arm gets broken and you're more worried about the rest of us losing a few days through down-time. I don't know what you call it, but to me, that's tough."

Trask decided to change the subject.

"I see that prick Cliff smacked Natalie again while I was gone," he offered, taking a sip.

Jorgensen grinned. Beneath his gruff exterior, Trask was a soft touch. The only people he didn't genuinely like were real assholes like Natalie's husband, Cliff. You had to earn Frank's enmity by being a total shit—and if you did, you had a hell of a time getting him to give you a second chance.

"If I was twenty years younger, I'd kick that miserable sonofabitch's ass," Trask growled, the muscles in his jaw pulsing as he ground his teeth in anger.

"Man, if I was twenty years younger, I'd spend two weeks at Mustang Ranch getting my ashes hauled all the way to Winnemucca and back," Habersham offered blandly.

Everybody laughed.

"Oh, man!" Ferdie said as he used his pocket handkerchief to wipe tears of laughter from his eyes. "Say, you know what? I think you could probably take Cliff even now, Frank. He's about your height and weight, even if he is younger than you. I remember when you backhanded the biker with the Mohawk two years ago. You know, the guy that was bothering Krystal? That guy must have had 40 pounds on you and six inches of reach."

Trask scowled at the memory. Krystal Calloway was the cocktail waitress on weekends. She was full of energy and ambition, supporting a ten-year-old son on the tips she earned at the bar. Ever since she had started at Pete's, he'd wished he'd had a daughter like her. Of course, if you want to win the lottery, you have to buy a ticket, and Frank had never married.

He admired women like Krystal and Natalie. They faced the worst the world could hand them without whining about it. They weren't complainers like some men he'd known. To Trask, they were the tough ones.

Jorgensen chuckled. "That was one surprised sonofabitch. I didn't know you could move that fast, Frank: Bam—quick as a fucking snake. He went backwards off his stool and cracked his head on the floor. I think there's still a mark there in the linoleum where he hit."

"That's only because nobody here ever mops the place," Habersham said with distaste.

Ferdie and Jorgensen both laughed again.

Trask sighed. "Yeah, you guys can yuk it up now, but it wasn't so funny when the cops showed up. That goon got a concussion. He could have died. I thought they were gonna charge me with felony assault."

"Yeah, but everybody saw him provoke it," Brundage said. "He had his hands all over Krystal, even after she told him to piss off. The cops finally got it sorted out and left you alone."

"Yeah," Habersham said. "And he hasn't been back since, either. I think he's afraid if he runs into you again, you'll kill him."

Trask allowed himself a small smile. "I'd do it again in a New York minute if I had to. I hate seeing a prick get away with stuff. Since I'm a short timer now, maybe I ought to carry a gun like Bill here does and start wasting these street punks. Do a Charlie Manson on 'em, like *Death Wish*, that picture he was in."

"You mean Charlie Bronson, Frank," Ferd said with a grin. "But when you get your blood up, oh, man! You're a little bit like Charlie Manson, too— kind of crazy, if you know what I mean."

***

Frank slept in his skivvies so when he heard the knock on his door at 3 a.m., he had to pull on his pants to see who was there. To his surprise, it was Natalie, in her nightgown, robe and slippers. She looked like she had already been crying for a while and was getting ready for more.

"Hey, kid," he said gently, "what's wrong?"

"Mr. Trask, I hate to bother you, but it's the baby," she said, her lower lip quivering. "She's got a horrible fever. I'm afraid she's d-dying." At her last word she burst into tears, her narrow shoulders shaking as she sobbed.

"Now, now," he said, putting his arm around her. "Where's your husband?"

"Cliff went out of town again looking for another job," she said between sobs. "I wouldn't bother you, but I have... nobody else..."

"Let's see her, Natalie," Trask said, steering her back toward her apartment.

The baby was barely stirring. Frank put his hand on her forehead and she was burning up. He gave a low whistle.

"We have to get her to the hospital, like right now, Natalie," he said. "Whatever is wrong with her is serious."

The distraught young woman sobbed even more violently. "But I have no money, no car.".

He put his hands on her shoulders. "Don't worry, kid," he said. "I'll have Mrs. Hung call us a cab. You get some street clothes on while I put on my shoes and grab my coat."

***

The intake staff at Highland must have had a soft spot for kids. They bumped Lucy up to the front of the queue waiting for treatment, so she skipped ahead of the other thirty people in the emergency room. The nurse practitioner called in a duty physician after the toddler registered a 105-degree temperature. Frank waited in the ER lobby while Natalie and the baby were hustled into a treatment room.

The clock on the wall said it was 6:17 a.m. He yawned; he probably would have been getting up in another hour anyway. *This hospital coffee is piss*, Frank decided, pouring most of his second cup down the drinking fountain drain with a scowl.

Down the hall, Natalie emerged from the treatment room talking with a young black woman in greens. They walked slowly toward the lobby together and Trask realized the other woman was his own Dr. Johnson.

"Don't you ever go home?" he asked her as they stopped in front of him.

"Sometimes," she said, giving him a weary smile. "All I have waiting for me there is my cat, and all she cares about is having me open one of her little cans of food."

Natalie had the confused look of somebody who had walked in during the middle of a conversation.

"Do you two know each other?" she asked.

Frank smiled. "Yeah, our season tickets to the ballet are right next to each other. She keeps sneaking my popcorn when she thinks I'm not looking."

Natalie looked even more confused.

"No, Natalie," he said with a laugh. "I just met her here the other day. She's my doctor."

"Are you okay, Mr. Trask?" Natalie asked.

Frank waved a hand. "Yeah, no problem," he said, winking the physician to silence. "I was just in for a checkup, that's all."

"What are you doing here?" Dr. Johnson asked.

Frank nodded at Natalie, who seemed on the verge of collapse. "I brought her," he said. "She lives next door and she didn't have cab fare. I figured whatever was going on with Lucy wasn't going to wait until the 57 bus started running this morning. How is she?"

The doctor turned to Natalie, smiled and squeezed her hand. "She'll be fine," she said. "It's a simple viral infection. Her fever should break in an hour or so."

Frank felt relief. He knew nothing about babies, so he assumed the worst when they got sick.

"We're going to keep her here for a day or so to make sure no complications set in," Johnson said. "A 105-degree temperature in a child is pretty frightening. You were right to bring her in."

"How are you doing?" the doctor asked.

He shrugged. "You told me I'm dying," he said, keeping his voice low to avoid alarming Natalie. "I guess I'm pretty doing good for somebody with one foot in the grave."

She sighed and glanced at her watch. "I have

to get back," she said. She put her hands on Natalie's shoulders. "Why don't you go home and get some rest, honey? You worry me more than your baby does. How did you get the big bruise on your eye?"

Natalie touched her shiner as if she'd forgotten it was there. "Oh, this?" she said. "I, uh—I walked into a door."

"Girlfriend, you have *got* to watch out for those doors," Johnson said, glancing at Frank in a way that made it clear she didn't believe a word of it. Frank shrugged to show he didn't believe it either.

"Take her home, would you, Mr. Trask?" Johnson said. "She can come back tomorrow afternoon after she's had some rest. Lucy will be in the pedo ward."

"Sure," Frank said as the doctor turned and strode back down the hallway of the ER, disappearing into another treatment room. He smiled to himself. For some reason, he liked it that she remembered his name.

***

Frank reluctantly got up around noon and after a shower, shave, a soft-boiled egg and coffee, decided to pay his money a visit at the credit union. He wanted to check the balance on the VA and savings accounts to see what they totaled.

Malea Ticsun, the nice middle-aged lady at the

counter, told him he could easily access his account information on his home computer. He told her he didn't have a home computer. When she said he could use the one at the public library, he held up his hand.

"Ms. Ticsun, I'm 67 years old," he said. "I've never sat down behind a computer. It took me two months to get straight on how to use the ATM machine. So could you please just tell me what my balance is?"

She left for a moment and came back with a computer printout. "Here you are Mr. Trask," she said, pronouncing it "mee-ster" in a way that reminded him she was from the Philippines.

"This is up to date," she said handing him his latest statements. "But it does not include interest for the last two days. Also, it weel not show any deposits or withdrawals you have made since midnight."

"That's okay." Frank smiled. "I haven't made any since midnight, anyway. Thanks a lot, ma'am."

As he glanced at the spreadsheet, she prattled on, talking about something called a Roth-IRA and reminding him that the credit union manager had talked him into transferring his straight savings accounts into a pair of them a couple of years earlier.

She enumerated the tax advantages they offered and gave him a lot of other technical information he would have needed a business degree to understand. The one thing she said that he did follow was that he could withdraw the money at any time without any penalties because the taxes on it had already been paid.

The bottom line was good: altogether, the VA and savings money totaled $442,389 and change. Plus there was an additional $15,000-plus in a small account he'd forgot opening when he and his buddies got a bonus in 1987 for breaking all the company's productivity records without a single industrial accident.

Frank could take a long trip with that kind of dough. Well, maybe not such a *long* trip, considering he was day-to-day, but a luxurious one, anyway. He could go to Europe and live it up in fancy hotels until he croaked. Or he could buy something really nice, some new clothes or something. The things he could do seemed limitless, even if the time he had left wasn't.

He was turning toward Pete's to read the paper and have a beer when he saw the stoop boys from next door sitting with a brown paper bag between them, laughing about something. Bob spotted Frank and gave Lenny a nudge, pointing Trask out. They both jumped to their feet leaving the bag on the steps behind them.

"Hey, Pops!" Lenny said. "You okay?"

Trask looked at him suspiciously. "Why? Are

you looking to borrow some money?"

"Fuck no, man," Lenny said, looking a little bit embarrassed. "I was just wondering, you know, how you're feeling and all?"

"I'm okay, kid," Frank said. "Why? What's up?"

"Ferdy, that guy that lives in the apartment building with you," Bob said. "He told us you got some kind of liver disease. He said you were real sick and had to go to the county hospital. Len and me, we were just worried about you is all."

Trask smiled tightly. He wanted to kill Ferd for putting his shit out on the corner like that. He should have been clearer about wanting to keep his condition quiet.

"Boys, don't sweat it," he said. "I'm okay. Ferdy just overdramatizes stuff, that's all. I'll probably live long enough to put both of you meatballs underground."

Lenny patted him on the shoulder. "I thought it might be something like that," he said but his skeptical smile showed he was unconvinced. Lenny and Bob weren't as dumb as Frank had thought they were.

"Well, if you need anything, let us know, huh old timer?" Lenny said. "You know—groceries picked up, whatever. Hate for you to get a hernia or something doing a bunch of bending or lifting."

"Yeah, man," Bob said. "You need something, let us know. You got a lot of friends around here, man. Hell, you're one of the few people I even like in this damned neighborhood."

To Frank's surprise, the two stoop boys insisted on shaking his hand. As they parted, Lenny pulled out a napkin from the burger joint up San Pablo and blew his nose into it, then stuck it back in his jeans.

"You take care of yourself, you hear?" he said, as he gave Frank another pat on the shoulder.

Trask smiled and nodded, then walked toward the tavern.

***

Inside Pete's, Trask put some Creedence and Rolling Stones on the box, breaking a Jackson to give him enough money for a long music session. The first of the old-timers to appear was Sam Jorgensen.

"I'm going to kill that fucking Gonzales," Frank said as Jorgensen took a seat.

"Why?" Sam asked.

"He's been crepe-hanging me all over the damned neighborhood. I just got stopped by a couple of knuckleheads who sit out on the step next door every day. They acted like I was about to croak. They were feeling so damned sorry for me I felt like crying myself!"

Jorgensen smiled. "So does it surprise you that

a bunch of people like you, you dumb bastard? Wake up and smell the bacon. You may be a sarcastic sonofabitch, but you got a shit-pot full of friends."

Trask snorted. "I just better not see any premature obituary notices in the paper, Sam. I'm not ready to go yet."

"How you feeling today?"

"Tired. I was up most of the night taking Natalie and Lucy to the hospital. Why do you ask?"

"You look tired, is all."

"Don't *you* start babying me now, okay?" Frank said. "For Christ's sake, I'm not some delicate piece of china that's about to break. I'm planning to live my life the way I always have until it's through. I don't want people acting like I'm their damn invalid aunt or something."

Jorgensen held up his hands. "All right. But you're asking me to act like nothing has happened when it damn well has. You're just about my best friend in the world. I hate the idea of you not being in it anymore."

Trask was touched. He stretched his right hand out across the table and Jorgensen clasped it. Trask wrapped his left hand over their grip. "Look, man, I feel the same way about you, but this is just a part of life, okay? This shit happens. Get used to it."

Jorgensen smiled, but Trask could see tears well in his eyes. "I don't think I'm going to get used to it, buddy," he said, quietly.

"Well, then," Frank said gruffly, clearing his throat. "If you're going to sit around thinking about me dying, help me figure out what to do in my final days. I got a little bit of money saved up. I'm trying to figure out how to spend it."

He had decided he would be vague about the size of his bankroll until he decided what to do with it. The possibility that his long-time friends would all start hoping to finagle their share, remote as it was, disgusted him. He wanted to remember them the way they were before he had a big bankroll and no time to spend it.

"What do you have in mind?" Jorgensen said, wiping his eyes hurriedly and blowing his nose.

"I don't really know," he said. "I've been thinking about it all afternoon. I started out with the idea maybe I should take a trip. You know: see Europe or something."

"You ever been out of the country besides 'Nam?" asked Jorgensen, who'd been in the 101st Airborne himself.

"Nope. Uncle Sam gave me a free trip to the Jolly Green Jungle and that's it."

Jorgensen thought about it. "Where do you most want to go?"

"Problem is, I don't really want to go anywhere."

"Why not?"

"I'm not going to know anybody when I get there," Frank replied, spreading his hands. "Everybody I know is here. I see you guys just about every day and you're the closest thing to a family I've got."

It was true. Since Gladys had died, Frank was the sole remaining member of the Trask bloodline. He didn't have another relative in the world—at least, not that he knew of.

"You'd meet new friends."

"I go someplace, everybody who sees me is going to know I'm an old fart from the U-S-of-A," he said. "Who's going to want to waste their time talking to some old American retiree? They'd probably think if they struck up a conversation, I'd spend the whole time bitching about taxes and how much money the government wastes. Either that or they're gonna start giving me shit about all the damn wars we're in.

"Nope," Trask said with assurance, shaking his head. "I don't think travel is going to ring my bell."

"Well, why don't you buy yourself something, then?" Jorgensen said. "How about a fancy new car?"

Trask laughed. It was a dry bark like the kind

made by one of the sea lions at that pier in San Francisco.

"That's a great idea except for one thing."

"Yeah, like what?"

"I don't have a license."

Jorgensen stared at him. "You got to be shitting me."

"It's true. I got busted a third time for driving drunk a few years ago and that was all she wrote. Permanent revocation. They wouldn't let me behind the wheel if I got put in charge of the Highway Patrol."

"I guess a car's out, then," Jorgenson said. "How about some new duds?"

Trask crossed his arms on his chest. "That was my second great idea. But where would I wear them? I never go anywhere. Just my apartment, that mom and pop the Arabs run across the street or this dive. Besides, I would just start to get them broken in about the time that I croaked. No sense in buying some nice outfits for St. Vincent de Paul; I'd be better off giving them the money directly and letting them buy what they need."

Jorgensen had no answer for that.

Trask sighed again. "I dunno," he said. "I just can't figure out what to do with this cash."

Sam brightened. "Hey, that St. Vincent de Paul idea isn't a bad one. Why don't you give the money to charity?"

Trask considered this. The notion had already occurred to him.

"That has possibilities, but I'd have to think about it. I don't want to piss it away on some outfit that will spend it all on salaries and perks for the bosses. I understand a lot of charity organizations roll that way. I'd want my money used to help people, not fatten up bureaucrats."

"Whatever, man," Sam told him with a smile. "I think you have the right idea, though."

Trask cocked an eye at him. "Yeah? How's that?" he asked.

Jorgensen spread his hands. "If you use your money in a way that makes you happy, that's one thing you'll never regret."

***

Bill and Ferdie came in soon afterward. Trask gave Ferd a hard time about letting it out that he was dying and Gonzales apologized, saying he'd asked the stoop twins not to run their mouths about it. Then the three of them spent an hour or so chatting before Frank, still groggy after his late night trip to the hospital with Natalie and Lucy, decided he needed to get more sleep. He stopped for some gumbo and soft crusted French bread from the soul food joint and when he returned to the Carlson, a city paramedic wagon was out in front, lights flashing. It pulled away from the curb with its siren beginning to wail as he climbed the front steps.

Mrs. Hung was at the entrance, wringing her hands.

"What's up, Mrs. Hung?" he asked as he watched the vehicle speed off. "Is somebody sick?"

"Somebody injured, Missah Trask," she said with concern, making the "R' in his last name so it sounded like an "L."

"Who got hurt?" he said, the hair on the back of his neck beginning to stand on end.

"Mizz Natarie," the landlady said. "She hurt bad. Real bad."

"Natalie? What happened to Natalie?"

Mrs. Hung shrugged, her expression one of deep concern. "Mr. Criff tell paramedic she fall down stairs. But her husband a bad man, very bad. I think he beat her up again."

Her words made Trask feel like throwing up.

"What makes you say that?"

"He was yelling in their apartment," she said. "He call out your name. Then their door slam. Mrs. Compton find her on second floor landing when she come back from grocery store."

Trask ground his teeth. He stopped himself when he realized Mrs. Hung was looking at him strangely because she could hear it. It was a good thing Lucy was in the hospital. He hated to think what Hatfield might have done to the child.

"Mrs. Hung, why don't you evict that bastard? If he keeps this up, he's going to kill her."

She sighed. "I throw him out, what happen to her and the baby? She afraid to leave him. They all just go someplace else where he do the same thing again. What good that do? At least here, some of us look after her a little."

She looked at Trask with resignation. "It not her fault he a big asshole."

Trask couldn't help but smile. Mrs. Hung might not be the most expert English speaker in the apartment house, but she was quite adept at using obscenity.

"Well, something has to be done," he said. "Sooner or later he's going to hurt her so badly the docs won't be able to fix her up. And then little Lucy will be at his mercy."

Trask trudged up the stairs to his flat. As he did, he remembered the two dirtbags that had murdered his sister: worthless scum that hadn't given a minute's thought to gunning down a woman old enough to be their mother. They were exactly like Natalie's rotten husband. The only real difference was, the person he kept edging closer to killing wasn't some stranger—it was his own wife.

There was just no two ways about it: some people were so rotten the world would be a better place without them.

Then, on the third floor landing, about a yard away from the stairs, he spotted a large dark stain almost in the center of the worn runner. Trask bent down to look at it. He touched it tentatively with his finger and found that it was still damp.

And red.

He realized it was what was left of a pool of Natalie's blood. She had been injured before she ever got to the stairs.

Trask stood, grinding his teeth again, clenching his fists at his sides. Now he knew exactly what he was going to do with the big wad of money in the credit union.

But he would get to that later. He had something else to take care of, first.

***

Trask waited until a little before 9 p.m. By then it was dark outside and the people who lived in the Carlson were mostly settled in their apartments. He opened his door quietly and checked the hallway. Nobody was moving around downstairs and the corridor was empty.

Moving quietly to the balustrade on the landing, he put his hand on the rail, testing it for give. It moved back and forth easily. The rail appeared to be glued to the individual balusters, probably with a pin at the top of each post that fit into a socket on the underside of the rail. That didn't matter; it was the newels at each end of the landing that supported the rail, not the balusters, which were mostly for show. What made the railing so dangerous was that it was barely secured at the anchor post nearest to the stairway to the second floor. The post was the only thing keeping it from collapsing when someone pushed it.

Trask moved to the newel. With both hands, he gave the rail a sharp tug where it connected and felt the lower end of the post pull away from the flooring. The pin holding it in place was rotten and it broke off with a dusty crunch, like a piece of dry toast being snapped in two. Trask shook the rail—it now swung more than a foot either way without resistance. He gently moved the rail back to its original position. When he let go, the entire balustrade quivered like jelly.

He looked at his hands and realized they were shaking, too.

Outside the Hatfield flat he steeled himself for a moment before giving the door three raps. After a minute it opened and Cliff Hatfield appeared, barefoot, wearing chinos and one of those sleeveless undershirts the kids call a "wife beater."

That's appropriate, Trask thought, sizing up the younger man. *A wife beater for a wife beater. Fucking perfect.*

Frank smelled the liquor as soon as Hatfield opened the door. He clearly had been drinking for some time, and judging from his bloodshot eyes, he'd been pounding the booze down at a rapid clip.

Hatfield seemed wobbly and steadied himself by leaning against the door jamb with one shoulder as he glared at Frank with unconcealed loathing.

Ferd was right about Cliff being Frank's height. But he outweighed Trask by a good thirty pounds and was close to 40 years younger. The younger man's face showed no trace of guilt, remorse, or regret.

You fucking psychopath.

"What is it, old man?" Hatfield said. "Make it snappy, huh? I was just getting ready to go visit my wife at the hospital. What do you want?"

Frank looked at him with contempt. "I'll bet you were," he said. "That's why you're all dressed up in your Sunday clothes. Don't worry, sonny boy. I won't take much of your precious time. I just wanted to stop by so I could get a good look at the face of a chickenshit bastard who enjoys hitting women, that's all."

For a moment, Hatfield looked confused—he couldn't believe the old man was talking to him with such fearless contempt.

"You're as yellow as baby shit, Hatfield," Trask added. "A real school bus. Scumbags like you are the best argument in the world for abortion. I take your wife to the hospital because your baby girl is sick and you go ballistic on her because another man did her a favor. Were you afraid she was going to run off with me, pissant? She should, you know. At least I have a set of balls."

Frank clocked the anger swelling in Hatfield's face. He wasn't quite there yet, though.

"Why don't you take a swing at a man for a change, you shitbird?" Trask said quietly. "Or are you too gutless to hit someone your own sex?"

Hatfield's blood rage was climbing quickly now. He had almost reached the point of homicidal fury.

"I thought so," Trask said, sneering at him with disgust. "No *cojones*. You make a fucking earthworm look like a sackful of balls, you spineless piece of shit."

Hatfield had reached the red zone. He cocked his fist and lunged forward with a curse. As he did, Frank, who could still move astonishingly fast for a senior citizen, took a half step to Hatfield's right and used both hands to give him a hard shove toward the balustrade. Cliff hit the rail with his stomach and grabbed it in desperation, trying to keep from going over.

If the rail had been properly anchored, he might have succeeded. Instead, the entire balustrade swung loose and arced into the stairwell; Cliff, his hands locked on the railing, went with it, leaving a howl of sudden terror hanging behind him.

With his heart pounding, Frank looked over the empty space where the balustrade had been. Hatfield was sprawled four stories below in a supine position, his body embedded in the tiny tiles that covered the lobby floor.

For some reason, Frank couldn't see the younger man's head and he wondered for a moment whether it had been torn off during the fall. Then he realized that the impact had splattered most of it across the floor above Cliff's shoulders.

Frank went back inside his apartment, directly to the toilet, knelt as if he was going to say a prayer and threw up everything he'd eaten that day.

***

Trask got lost twice at Highland the next afternoon but a nurse who was going off-duty took pity on the old geezer with the vase full of flowers in one hand and the little suitcase in the other and guided him to Natalie's room.

When he entered he found Natalie sitting up in bed, holding Lucy. She was smiling slightly, despite the cast on one arm and new bruises on her mouth and jaw. When she saw Frank, her smile widened.

"That's the sweetest thing I've ever seen," he

said with a grin as he set the flowers on the table beside her and put the suitcase next to his feet. "How are both of you doing?"

"She's well enough to go home," she said. "But they aren't going to release me until they finish looking at the X-rays of my leg."

"Your leg?" Frank said, his tone making it a question.

"It got twisted when Cliff... when I fell down the stairs," she said, biting her lip. "They want to make sure that it isn't broken. I suppose... I guess Cliff will have to take her," she added, a cloud of worry crossing her face.

Frank swallowed. "Didn't anybody tell you?"

She looked puzzled. "Tell me what?"

"It's your husband. I thought somebody from the police would have stopped by already to let you know. Cliff... Well, Cliff had an accident. You know that loose rail on the third floor landing I warned you about?"

She stared at Frank without speaking. He could tell from her expression she knew exactly what had happened.

"Apparently nobody warned Cliff," he continued. "It collapsed on him last night and he fell all the way to the lobby. He broke his neck in the fall. Fractured his skull, too. The paramedics got there a few minutes after he fell, but there was nothing they could do. I'm afraid he was already gone, Natalie."

She leaned back into the pillows with her eyes closed. Tears rolled down her cheek.

"I'm sorry, kiddo," Frank said.

"I am too, Mr. Trask," she said in a voice that was almost a whisper.

Frank swallowed again. "Natalie, I found blood on the carpet on the third floor landing," he said, fumbling for the words. "You were bleeding before you fell down the stairs. Cliff hit you, didn't he?"

She nodded.

"And you didn't just fall, did you?" he asked.

Her lips formed the word "No," but her answer was too quiet to hear.

"Cliff threw you down those stairs, didn't he? That black eye you have; did he do that?"

Her answer was a sob that shook her entire body. She didn't need to add anything.

Frank said nothing for a moment.

"Why did you stay with him when he hurt you so many times?" he asked finally.

With her tears still streaming down her face, she gave him a soft smile, as if remembering something nice someone had done for her many years ago.

"You may find this hard to believe, Mr. Trask, but he was a wonderful man when we first got married," she said, her voice barely audible. "He was kind, considerate. Then he lost his job. And when I first got pregnant with Lucy a little more than a year ago, he started to change. I don't know what happened. I hoped he would snap out of it, but he never did."

She paused as memories crowded her mind. "He would sit and look at me for hours without saying anything," she added, closing her eyes in pain as she relived the last twelve months. "Then he started going out and getting drunk, almost every night. The first time he hit me was when he came back from the bar one night and I asked him what was wrong. He said he couldn't trust me anymore. He said he thought the baby growing inside me wasn't his, that I had sex with somebody when he was gone looking for a new job. He called me all sorts of names."

Frank spread his hands. "Everybody in the building knew he was beating you. Why didn't you ask us for help?"

"I kept hoping he would change," she said so quietly he could barely hear. "I kept hoping he would get better."

Then she burst into tears again, crying in racking sobs.

Trask was amazed by some people's capacity for love, even in the face of unbelievable cruelty.

He picked up the suitcase and put it on the bed beside her and the baby.

"Natalie," he said. "You and Lucy are on your own now. You have to start over. I want you to take what's in this suitcase; it will help you make a new beginning."

Then he went away and left her with her baby and her grief.

***

"Oh, man!" Ferdie said, excitedly. "How much money was in that case again?"

"Four hundred grand," Trask said, sipping his Seven and Seven. "That'll keep them going for a while. She's going to be all right. If she could take all the shit that asshole was handing out, she can get back on her feet with the help of that money."

"Jesus," Habersham said. "With four hundred gees, I really could get my ashes hauled to Winnemucca and back. Hell, I could buy into Mustang Ranch and get the shareholder discount!"

Trask grinned. "If you spent all $400,000 on Viagra, you probably couldn't get hard enough to put on a condom, Bill."

Even Habersham joined the laughter this time.

"So you just got this idea on the spur of the moment when you heard this girl's old man had croaked?" Jorgensen asked. "Right out of the clear blue sky?"

His voice had the same edge it might if Trask had offered him a deed to the Golden Gate Bridge.

Trask looked at him blandly, the picture of innocence. "Yeah. Just like that. Why?"

"Where were you when this shitbird fell, Frank?" Jorgensen asked.

Frank's face turned red. "I was in my room, Sam."

Jorgensen looked at him thoughtfully.

"It seems like an interesting coincidence to me," he said. "You find out you have all this money saved up; the girl's psycho husband sends her to the hospital; then the psycho just happens to fall 50 feet onto his neck in a freak accident a few hours later. The next day you give his widow your life savings. Lucky girl."

"Well, that's how it happened," Frank said testily. "Believe it or not."

"Whatever," Sam said. "It looks to me like she may have been more than lucky. Like maybe Lady Luck had a helper."

He and Trask locked eyes momentarily. Then Jorgensen smiled. "But that's all just speculation, of course."

Trask gave him a nervous look. "I hope you don't discuss your speculation with anybody else. Like the cops, for instance."

Jorgensen looked hurt. "Frank, you know I don't talk to cops."

"So what are you going to do with the rest of the money, Frank?" said Ferdie, who, like

Habersham, had no idea what Jorgensen and Trask were talking about.

Frank turned and signaled to Brundage at the bar. He came to the table carrying a tray of fresh drinks.

"I invested it in a local business," Trask said as Joe cleared away their dead soldiers. "As long as any of you jokers are still alive, you're drinking at Pete's courtesy of my new $57,389 tab. If you outlast my dough, you're on your own. Otherwise, when the last of us steel mill geezers is gone, Pete gets whatever's left."

"Now that's my kind of good deed," Habersham said.

Lifting his beer to eye level, Jorgensen gave Trask a wink and said, "Here's to good deeds— and to good luck, too!"

Trask raised his glass.

"I'll drink to that," he said with a smile. "For a little while longer, anyway."

THE CREEP

BY WILLIAM E. WALLACE

The Claymore apartment building where Susan Carnes lived was more than a century old and the 85-year-old "new" elevator it boasted seemed to work roughly three weeks of the year. Figuring out which weeks could be a challenge.

Most of the time Susan ended up climbing the rickety uneven staircase, watching closely to avoid the runner of paper-thin carpet that humped up under her feet like a booby trap.

She knew the dilapidated state of the building was why her rent came to only $250 a month. What she didn't understand was why half the lights on the landings were always out, since the electricity they consumed couldn't be that expensive. Whatever the reason, the resulting gloom always put Susan's nerves on edge.

They were on edge now, in fact.

As she turned the blind corner on the fourth floor landing, a cockroach racing over the riser distracted her so much that she almost ran into the man who lived in the studio directly above hers. He loomed out of the shadows like a very substantial ghost.

"Oh my God," she gasped. "I'm so sorry. I didn't see you coming."

It was the first time she had encountered her neighbor since he moved in three weeks earlier. Her neighbor Mrs. Riley had mentioned him, but Mrs. Riley mentioned a lot of things. Susan tended to ignore most of them.

"It's my fault, miss," he rasped, the rustle of his low voice like a breeze stirring the dry leaves in the Seventh Street cemetery six blocks away. It was a dead voice with the mechanical character of a recording that had been pieced together from different sounds, something like the machine that called out stops on the crosstown bus she rode to the hospital four days a week. Speaking seemed to pain the man and he coughed afterward, inclining his head and using the back of his left forearm to cover his mouth.

Susan stared at his hand—slick and shiny as a piece of paraffin and almost the same color. It seemed undersized for such a tall, wide-shouldered man, but she realized almost immediately that it was short because he seemed to be missing the first joints of each finger: the ends, nails and all, looked as if they had melted off.

She glanced up at his face. Only a strip of it showed between the turned-up collar of his military-issue raincoat and the lowered brim of his baseball cap. To her shock, she saw that it, too, had a melted, waxen look, like a dummy from the

72

museum near the bus station. But the dummy would need a long time in the summer sun to get that sheen.

The man's haunted pale gray eyes were the only natural-looking part of his face.

He nodded abruptly, squeezed next to the banister. The contents of the sack he carried clinked as he shifted it to give her more room. "Excuse me," he said as he passed.

His footsteps were heavy on the bare wood, as if his bag contained more than a batch of bottles. The droop to his shoulders, his slow trudge, the creak of the steps under his weight—they made it seem like he was lugging a lifetime of regret.

Susan half turned as he disappeared into the darkness above. "Christ!" she whispered to herself, realizing she had been holding her breath during the encounter. The man's scars—those she had seen, anyway—were frightening, like something from a horror movie.

She flew down the remaining three flights of stairs with her heart in her throat and was still trembling when she reached the Claymore's front entry.

***

"Have you seen that new guy who moved into the studio upstairs?" Sonny Jackson asked.

Marcel didn't answer. He was busy watching Bitsy, the girl with pink hair and a stud in her tongue who lived across the street. Bits was flaked out on her stoop, lounging back with her elbows on the riser behind her, knees up and legs wide apart. Her pose was exactly the same as Marcel's. She stared at him coolly and Marcel wasn't sure whether she was coming on to him or trying to show him up in front of his buddies.

She was chewing gum and blew a small, tight bubble, then looked at him defiantly when it burst. Definitely a come-on sort of look.

"Skank," Marcel said with a disdainful smile, shaking his head. "See that, what she did with the gum? That cunt would pay me to pack her fudge."

Two of the five youths sitting with Marcel laughed. Bitsy could tell she was being dissed so she rose with as much dignity as a person with pink hair could muster, flipped Marcel off and went back into her apartment building.

"What a boxer," Marcel called after her. "Woof, woof, baby! Go chase a car!"

"You screw her, you have to go to the vet, get a bath for fleas," said Oscar One-eye, a 21-year-old whose squint made him look like he was perpetually winking.

"Not fleas, man, worms," said Roger Heath. Roger, four months out of juvie, had been Marcel's number two until a few weeks ago when he said something that pissed Marcel off. He never figured out what it was but he'd been trying to work his way back into favor ever since.

Marcel turned to Sonny. "What did you say, man?"

Sonny was the only one in the group who hadn't laughed at Marcel's jibe or tried to top it by insulting Bits himself. Nobody expected him to: Sonny wasn't the brightest button on the blazer, but his loyalty was unquestioned. He would stand shoulder to shoulder with Marcel against any other gang on the west side of town, and had done so several times.

"I asked if you seen the new guy, the one upstairs who wears the hat and raincoat all the time," Sonny said. "I got a good look at him when he came back from Gloria's last night. He was all fucked up, man—drunk on his ass."

"You talking about G.I. Joe?" Marcel said.

Sonny frowned. "You mean one a those little soldier dolls?"

Marcel grinned and his entourage smiled with him, even though half of them had no idea what he was talking about. Didn't do to look like you were as dumb as Sonny around Marcel; automatically put you on his loser list and Marcel wouldn't trust you to peddle the chalk he scored from the beaners on 72nd Street, or do any of the other little jobs he pulled to make spending money.

"Yeah, Sonny," he said with a smirk. "Like the

little soldier dolls. Somebody told me the guy was in Afghanistan. Got his ass cooked when the truck he was in ran over some rag-head bomb."

Sonny's expression showed he was turning that information over in his head. Obviously took effort.

"I guess that would explain it, then," he said finally.

"Explain what?"

"Why the sonofabitch is so butt-ugly," Sonny said. "He's a real creep, man. Dude's got more scars than that guy in the Elm Street movies."

"You mean Freddie Krueger?" Oscar asked. He hadn't seen the new guy and was still trying to figure out why Sonny was talking about him.

"Yeah," Sonny said, smiling slightly. "The guy in those kids' dreams. With the claw for a hand."

"It's not a claw, Sonny," Roger said, trying to work his way into the discussion. "It's more like a set of knives or something."

"Yeah—Ginzus!" said Oscar. "They slice, they dice, they make millions of julienne fries—out of teenagers."

"Whatever," Sonny said with a shrug. He wasn't a stickler for details. "Anyways, the guy is as big as a horse, I swear to God. Like my uncle Stevie, only bigger."

The members of Marcel's clique exchanged glances. If Sonny wasn't just talking shit, this G.I.

guy must be huge. Steve Riggins was the biggest
man any of them had ever seen outside of a cage
match on TV. He'd played football in high school
and was all-state, a probable scholarship candidate,
until he was expelled for selling the other players
reefer. He worked as a longshoreman and looked
like he could lift the business end of a Volkswagen
bug without breaking a sweat.

"You sure about that, Sonny?" Marcel asked.
"Is he really bigger than Stevie?"

"I ain't lying, boss," Sonny said. "He got scars
like Freddie Krueger but he looks more like
Frankenstein."

"You mean the monster," said Luis Cardeña,
the resident wise ass.

"What?" Sonny looked confused.

"The monster," Cardeña said. Luis had once
read a book. That made him a Mensa candidate
compared to the other stoop boys.

"Frankenstein was the scientist, some little
skinny-assed dude," he said. "The guy he stitched
together from corpses was the monster."

Obviously, the book he'd read wasn't the one
by Mary Shelley.

"What the fuck ever," Marcel said with
irritation. He decided he'd have to slap the shit
out of Luis sometime—asshole was way too big
for his britches.

The other guys started telling each other

stories about Stevie Riggins's feats of strength, but Marcel was thinking about the new man living upstairs. A guy that big in the building could be trouble, he thought. There was only room for one alpha dog in the Claymore and Marcel was it. He would have to keep an eye out for this big-assed ex-soldier.

***

"It was creepy, Millie," Susan said as she loosely folded soiled bedding and placed it into the laundry cart. St. Bartholomew's was short-handed and the two RNs had been asked to help with the domestic chores. "Seriously creepy. He scared the hell out of me, coming out of the dark like that."

Millie Howard, the orderly who worked with her in the hospital's southwest wing, pulled the sheets and the rubber liner off the bed on the opposite side of the empty ward.

"What was it that scared you?" She wadded the linen, put it in the cart and deposited the liner in a canvas bag. "Was it the way he looked or the way he suddenly appeared in front of you?"

Susan thought a moment. "I dunno," she said. "I think the way he showed up all of a sudden startled me to begin with. I didn't see his face or hand until he spoke, so it couldn't have been the way he looked, except for his size."

Millie paused, holding a sheet in her hands.

"How big was he?"

"Big. When I first saw him, he was at least a step below me but I still had to look up at him."

"That's pretty tall," she said. "What was it he said to you again?"

"Something like, 'Sorry, Miss.'" Susan tried to remember the incident as accurately as possible. "No, wait. That wasn't it. He said, 'My fault, Miss.' That's all. And 'Excuse me' as he passed."

Millie smiled. "At least he has manners. Did he sound like he was, you know, pissed off or anything?"

"No, he just moved over and squeezed by. He even moved the bag he was carrying so that it hung over the banister, out of my way." Now, in the brightly lit ward, talking to her friend about it, Susan wondered why she had found her neighbor so frightening.

"Hm."

"I'm being silly, aren't I?" Susan said, smiling. "Making a big deal out of nothing, really. He was perfectly nice to me. He was just big...and horribly scarred."

"Yeah," Millie said, frowning. "I wonder what happened to him to make him look that way?"

Susan bit her lip as she realized that thought had never entered her mind. She had been so caught up in her surprise and fear that she hadn't felt any sympathy for the poor man. Working at

St. Bart's she saw lots of people who were in bad shape but she couldn't remember ever seeing anybody who looked as bad as the man on the stairs. At least, not that was still alive.

"I don't know," she said, wondering if she was losing her ability to empathize with other people. She heard that could happen, working in an emergency ward all day with men and women who had been cut, stabbed, shot, whatever. "What is it you call those thick scars that make your skin look like wax? You know—excessive collagen formation in the corium?"

Millie stripped another bed. "Keloid scars," she said. "Sounds like burns. I worked at Northeast in the burn ward for a year and a half when I first got hired here at the hospital. There were several people in there with scars like the ones you've described. Most of them had already had a lot of skin grafts and reconstructive surgery to try and repair the damage. The scar tissue was thick and slick looking, like it was wet. It sort of looked like they were melting right in front of you."

Susan made a face. "Burns that bad must be terribly painful," she said, belatedly feeling pity for the man on the stairs.

"No kidding," Millie said. "Most of the victims in northeast were taking painkillers. Morphine and other strong stuff."

THE CREEP

***

"You've been self-medicating again, Mr. Baldocchi," Dr. Clinton Smith said with a look of dismay.

Stripped to the waist, Alan Baldocchi felt edgy and self-conscious. The waxy scars that covered his body from his knees to the crown of his head were hideous. Normally he did everything he could to conceal them, wearing his shirt collar buttoned to the top, the collar of his raincoat turned up and his cap tugged down to cover most of his head and face.

When Smith examined him he had to strip away this disguise, revealing the pasty featureless mass underneath what had once been normal tissue. Baldocchi's routine bitterness intensified on those occasions; he became even more snide and sarcastic than usual.

"Did that show up in the lab work you keep ordering for me?" he asked the doctor. His voice was as rough as coarse sandpaper on a piece of old wood.

"I didn't need any tests," Smith said. "I can smell it on you. Anybody who drinks that much, the alcohol starts to seep out of their pores."

Baldocchi tried to smile but the scar tissue around his mouth wasn't flexible enough. Also he was fighting off the miserable headache his hangover had left behind. The pain in his skull made demonstrations of humor difficult.

"I still have pores?" he said. "I would have thought they'd be burned off, like my hair, eyebrows and eyelashes."

Smith ignored the crack. "I told you before, you keep drinking like you do and you'll be dead in a few more years."

The big man with the scars shrugged. "Instead of being dead for the last two years, like I should have been in the first place."

Where he was sitting on the edge of the examination table, the mirror on the wall across from him made it impossible for him to avert his eyes from the claylike wound that was his skin. He wasn't used to this much illumination. Baldocchi kept the motley collection of table lamps in his flat at the Claymore turned off until he wanted to read something. He didn't mind the gloom; at least it helped conceal what he looked like. He shuddered.

"Can I cover this up?" he asked.

Smith nodded. "Have you seen Dr. Kennedy yet?"

Baldocchi pulled on his shirt. Kennedy was the psychiatrist Smith had referred him to for his post-traumatic stress disorder. "Yeah, I saw her."

"What did she say?"

"That I should stop drinking."

Smith frowned. "I meant about your... depression."

Baldocchi shrugged again. "She said I was depressed. I asked her if she knew why. She said no. I told her she'd be depressed, too, if she looked like I do."

Smith sighed. "It doesn't sound like it was a very fruitful consultation."

Baldocchi tried an ironic smile again, but had no more success than he'd had the first time. The scar tissue was too stiff to allow normal expressions; a grimace was all he could muster. It had to serve as his smile, his frown, his look of sympathetic concern.

"It was fruitful for her," he said. "She got paid for my visit. They do still pay you Veteran's Administration docs, don't they?"

"You know, you have a remarkably poor attitude for a man living on borrowed time."

"Maybe I don't like the interest rate on the loan," Baldocchi said. "I didn't ask to be a survivor and if I'd known how I was going to end up, I would have blown my brains out, myself."

"That's not very likely, Mr. Baldocchi. When they pulled you out of the Bradley, you were unconscious and in shock. You were barely alive. If it had taken a few minutes longer to get to you, you probably wouldn't have made it at all."

"Lucky me," Baldocchi said. He'd had this

conversation with the doctor before. It bored him.

"Tell me, when do you usually start hitting the bottle?" Smith asked.

Baldocchi thought about it. He didn't really want to answer. Like most out-of-control drinkers, he didn't like thinking about how much alcohol he consumed.

"I usually wait until the sun is over the yardarm," he said, finally. "Generally not before 5 p.m."

The doctor gave him a skeptical look.

Baldocchi snorted. "It's after five p.m. someplace all the time."

"And you drink until, what? Closing time?"

Baldocchi nodded. "Generally, yes."

"Why don't you do something else for a change? Go to a movie. Read a book."

Baldocchi grunted. "Fact is, I'm reading a book, right now. I even take it to the local bar with me."

Smith looked at him dubiously. "Yeah? What are you reading?"

"It's something by a guy named Hubert Selby," Baldocchi said. "It's called *Last Exit to Brooklyn.*"

Smith rolled his eyes. "That's a great picker-upper. And here I was wondering why you're always so damned melancholy. That book is one of the most depressing things I ever cracked. Why don't you read something lighter?"

Baldocchi shrugged. "I get absorbed in the characters in a book like *Last Exit*," he said. "What do you want me to read? *Brothers Karamazov*? *Mad* magazine? *Pride and Prejudice*?"

Smith snapped his fingers. "That's it, Jane Austen! Why don't you read *Pride and Prejudice*?"

"I did, two months ago. I'll tell you what's depressing—Elizabeth Bennet's stupid younger sisters. And that dumb bastard, Wickham."

Smith's blank look and fixed semi-smile told Baldocchi he had never read the book himself and had no idea who those characters were.

Baldocchi sighed.

The doctor stood. "Well, your physical health seems as good as could be expected," he said. "Except for your liver, anyway. You really need to stop drinking."

"Yeah, I know. You keep telling me so. But you don't tell me how I'm supposed to deal with getting up in the morning, looking in the bathroom mirror and seeing a monster stare back at me. How am I supposed to get used to that?"

Smith looked at him and shook his head. "There were nine men in that carrier and you're the only one who survived. A lot of people would look at you and call you a miracle. They'd say God saved you for a reason."

"Yeah?" Baldocchi snorted. "A lot more people would look at me and scream. I almost gave some young woman a heart attack coming up the stairs at the apartment house yesterday. I doubt she looks at me and sees a miracle. I'll bet what she sees is a walking horror show. Why not? It's how I see myself."

Baldocchi finished putting on his coat and picked up his cap. He held it for a second before pulling it on. It slipped down over the misshapen lumps at the sides of his head that had once been his ears.

"You know, God and I don't have much contact these days, doc, " he said. "Next time you talk to him, why don't you ask him what he saved me for, okay?"

He used the stubs of the fingers on his left hand to open the door, then turned back to Smith before passing through it. "I hope he tells you that it was for something other than frightening women and children."

***

Marcel was sitting at the top of the stoop with his band of stooges scattered around him when Susan got home to the Claymore after work.

"He-e-ey, baby," the gang leader said with a grin as she climbed the steps, fishing in her purse for her keys. He casually reached out and ran his hand down her leg from mid-thigh to just below the knee. His palm was rough and dry on Susan's pantyhose and she shuddered at his touch.

"How's my best girlfriend today?" he added, leering at her.

Susan didn't answer. Marcel Lanslie was only 23 or 24, about six years younger than Susan. Despite his tender years he was already known to his neighbors in the Claymore as a small-time thief, drug dealer, car booster, purse-snatcher and general purpose thug. His "posse," as he liked to call them, was a gang of juvenile delinquents. Marcel controlled them because he was smart, fearless and tough.

Not that he actually made much effort to control them.

He was also the leader of the pack because he was good-looking: until he got sent away to the juvenile prison for a couple of years he was the neighborhood heartbreaker, a movie-star handsome kid whose charisma surrounded him with young women trying to catch his eye. But at juvie he had mobbed up with the 14th Avenue Crips and by the time he paid his second visit to the place he was a full-blown 'banger.

Susan didn't know any of this, of course. When you moved into the Claymore, the super didn't give you copies of the other tenants' rap sheets. If he did, decent people would go someplace else and there wouldn't be anybody living there except parolees and prostitutes.

She found out some of Marcel's history from

neighbors, primarily Mrs. Riley, the apartment's gossip-in-chief. Susan had been inclined to give Marcel the benefit of the doubt when she first moved in—misunderstood kid, father absent from the home, mother a junkie and part-time streetwalker, etc. She tolerated his innuendo and pretended she thought he was playing for laughs. But being nice to him had only encouraged him to be more brazen and aggressive. After a while, she began ignoring him entirely. It didn't make him stop, however.

"Hey, don't be so stuck up," he said when she didn't answer, giving her calf a squeeze with his hand. "A guy's friendly to you, you're supposed to be friendly back."

She continued to dig in her hand bag as Marcel climbed to his feet and began walking alongside her. It was a terrible time to have trouble finding her keys: Marcel had been escalating his crude comments for the past couple of months, and last week he had touched her for the first time, putting his arm around her shoulder as she walked up the stairs.

Having to pass by him and his gang when she got off work had become a daily ordeal. Two days ago he had put his hand on her hip and leaned against the door while she tried to open it, whispering a crude suggestion in her ear then turning to grin at his underlings as they laughed at her discomfort.

He seemed to be working up to some sort of sexual confrontation. Whatever he had in mind wouldn't happen today, though.

"Hey, check it out," one of Marcel's minions said suddenly, gesturing down the street. "It's Freddy fucking Krueger himself!"

Susan looked up and saw the big man who lived above her moving slowly toward the apartment building.

"Hey, Freddy!" Marcel said, turning toward the scarred man with a grin. "Haunt anybody's dreams lately?"

She was glad the stoop boys had stopped tormenting her to pick on the burned man, but her relief also made her feel guilty. Susan found her keys and unlocked the door, but hesitated as the gang of neighborhood toughs taunted the man with the scars.

"Where's your hand with the blades, Freddy?" said one of them she knew as Sonny, grinning at his companions. "You forget and leave it on the bus or something?"

The big man said nothing as he climbed the stairs.

Marcel stepped onto the step above him, blocking his way, but the man with the scars still was tall enough to look directly in the gang leader's eyes.

"You should try to be a little friendlier, Freddy," Marcel said. "Get to know us better. We're just like family here."

He turned to Susan and winked. "Aren't we, gorgeous?"

The big man cleared his throat and murmured something to Marcel.

"What?" the hoodlum said. "Speak up, Freddy. I couldn't hear you."

The big man leaned toward Marcel until their faces were only inches apart.

"I said, 'stand aside before I hurt you,'" he replied in a voice that was scarcely more than a hoarse whisper.

There was no bravado to his comment, no false menace. It was simply a statement of fact, as if he'd said the front steps needed sweeping, or someone should pick up the trash in the street. The big man looked into Marcel's eyes; his stare as empty as a grave.

Marcel's smile disappeared, replaced by a look of shocked disbelief. Somehow, the big man's quiet words were as menacing as a declaration of war. Marcel moved back involuntarily and the man with the scars walked past without giving him a second look.

Susan stepped inside and held the door for the big man, who touched the bill of his cap in acknowledgement and rasped, "Thank you, miss."

As the scarred man entered, Marcel found his voice.

"Fucking creep," he sputtered in an angry squeak. "You better watch your ass, Freddy. Ima fuck you the hell up."

***

Susan woke up with a start, sitting straight up in her bed. She glanced at the clock on her side table and saw it was a few minutes after three in the morning. Then she heard the sound that had awakened her again: a low groan that oozed through the ceiling of her apartment.

The sound stopped abruptly and a hollow click a second later told her the man who lived upstairs had turned on a light. There was the sound of labored breathing, then she heard his low rasping voice, almost as if he was in her room.

"No, Commander, not the left branch, I said. Take the right. The right. The right. No—the right fork; there's something wrong with the road up there.

"Why won't you listen? I told you, there's something wrong, can't you see it? It's on the left, like, right there. Dirt piled up. It's on the left, damn it. Turn right. Turn right, damn you!

"Damn you!"

The last two words were more of a cry of anguish than actual speech, the guttural scream of a terrified man facing something much worse than death—something he had faced countless times before.

Silence followed. Eventually she heard the creak of springs as the man upstairs climbed out of bed, then a thump and a muffled curse as he banged into something in the dark. The clink of a bottle against a glass followed by the noisy glug, glug, glug of drinking. The man upstairs groaned again, apparently not conscious of making the sound, then poured and drank a second time. The liquid sound was easy for Susan to make out in the darkness of her flat.

He drained the glass a third time and bumped it on wood as he put it down. It scraped against the edge of the table then fell onto the floor with a clunk.

"The stupid bastards," he muttered. Then he began to cry with a racking sob that rattled deep inside his chest.

Susan lay in the dark, staring at the ceiling, listening until his sobs turned into a fitful snoring. Her own eyes were filled with tears when he finally drifted off. She couldn't get back to sleep herself for a long time afterward.

***

"Hey, I've been checking up on that guy with the scars," Susan told Millie over coffee in St. Bart's cafeteria. "His name is Alan Baldocchi."

"How'd you find that out?" Millie asked.

"I asked the Claymore's super this morning when I saw him in the hall. He told me that Mr. Baldocchi was an Army sergeant in Afghanistan. He got a medical discharge the last time he was wounded over there."

"Did the super know how it happened?"

"No, just that it was a combat thing. He said he only talked to the guy briefly. A rental agency sent him over to the apartment house. All he needed from the super was the key to his flat."

Millie smiled. "See? The other day you just thought he was some creep out of a horror picture. Now you know he's a vet. Maybe even a war hero."

Susan blushed. "I don't know about any heroics, but I was wrong about the creep thing, that's for sure. Actually, he seems to be really nice. I feel sorry for him. I heard him talking to himself in his room in the middle of the night. Something about a Captain and staying on the right. I don't know what it was about, but it really seemed to bother him."

She didn't mention that her neighbor cried himself to sleep. She was a little ashamed to have been listening, even though there was no way to avoid it since the Claymore had walls like tissue paper.

"Why don't you ask him?" Millie said.

Susan frowned. "What?"

"Why don't you ask him how he got so scarred?"

Susan bit her lower lip. "God, Mill," she said. "I don't really know the guy. I can't ask him something like that."

"Why not?" Millie asked. "You know his name, don't you?"

"Yeah, but I found out what it was by snooping, not because he told me or somebody introduced us."

Millie gave her a puzzled look. "So it's better somehow to sneak around behind his back than it is to just say 'Hi' and ask how he got injured? You tell me he seems to be a nice guy, so treat him like one. He's your neighbor, for Pete's sake. Maybe he'd enjoy having somebody to talk to."

That was Millie: blunt and to the point. Probably right, too, Susan thought.

"But what if he's one of those people who won't let you be once he finds out you're friendly?" Susan asked. "That guy I went out with a year ago turned out to be one of those—he spent all his time calling me after, dropping by the hospital to walk me home and stuff. He was like a damned stalker; I couldn't get shut of him."

"I guess you won't know what kind of person this Baldocchi is unless you talk to him, will you? So you end up spending some time being friendly with the guy? Big deal. It's not like you got much else going on in your life right now, anyway. You got nursing classes twice a week. You aren't dating anybody. You go to work and go home, watch a little TV and go to bed. What's it going to cost you to fit a couple of hours of being nice to an ex-G.I. into that busy schedule?

"Besides, you're supposed to be in the helping profession," Millie added with a crooked grin. "That doesn't mean you stop helping when you clock out of St. Bart's."

The way Millie put it made Susan feel ashamed.

"Okay, okay. I'll think about it. Now let's get back to work before the Ward Chief comes looking for us."

***

The timer went off 45 minutes after Susan put the macaroni and cheese into the oven. The recipe she used called for an hour of baking time but she took the enameled iron pan out early anyway. The gas range in her apartment was so old that the company that made it no longer existed; it never hurt to check something before it was supposed to be done. The oven was inclined to overcook things. When it wasn't undercooking them instead.

Tonight was a good example. When she put the casserole in the middle of the table in the kitchen to cool, she noticed that its edges had browned more than she intended. She sighed. It wasn't the kind of first impression she had hoped to make.

"He'll probably think I'm one of those women who can't boil water," she said to herself as she checked the dish for other flaws. She was pleased to note that the buttered bread crumbs on top were a golden brown and the cheesy sauce was bubbling the way it should.

"Well, it's just gonna have to do." She took off her apron and used hot mitts to place the casserole on a pair of plates that held a large serving spoon and two forks. She took a deep breath to steady her nerves, then picked up her offering and climbed the stairs to the next floor.

With her hands full, Susan had to use the toe of her shoe to knock on the door to Baldocchi's apartment.

"Yeah?" came the big man's hollow-sounding voice, followed by a dry cough that rattled inside his chest.

"Hi," she said through the closed door, blushing as she realized she really didn't know what to say. "It's Susan Carnes, the woman who lives downstairs. I'm the one who held the door for you yesterday—the one who almost ran you down on the stairs."

There was a moment of silence inside, then Baldocchi cleared his raspy throat. "Yes," he said.

"I remember. What can I do for you, Ms. Carnes?"

"Mr. Talmadge, the superintendent of the building, told me you live by yourself up here," she said. "I figured you might like a home-cooked meal, so I made you some mac 'n' cheese."

He was silent for so long she wondered if he was still there. Finally, she heard the sound of the latch inside being released and the squeak of the hinges as he opened the door to his flat.

Susan could see now that her recollection of how big he was had been wrong. He wasn't just big: he was immense. Standing straight up inside his apartment's doorway, he appeared to be nearly seven feet tall and almost a yard wide at the shoulders.

He had delayed opening the door so he could put on a cap and wrap a scarf around his neck and face. His shirt's long sleeves were buttoned shut at the bottom, exposing only his hands.

He saw her looking at his outfit. "I'm sensitive about how I look," he said. "I'm a mess, so I try to keep as much of myself covered as possible."

As he spoke, Susan caught an alcoholic whiff that smelled like whisky. She remembered the sound of him drinking alone the night she'd heard him crying. It made her wonder if all the bottles in the bag he had been carrying on the stairway had been liquor.

They locked eyes. Unlike most of the people he met, she didn't turn away and pretend she wasn't looking at him.

He gazed at her with curiosity. "Do my... my scars bother you?" he asked.

"I'm getting used to them," she said. "I'll be honest—you scared the hell out of me on the stairs the other day."

He winced at her candor, even though he had the same reaction sometimes when he suddenly saw his reflection in a mirror.

But then she continued: "I started to think about it afterward. I wondered why you had frightened me. After all, it's just your skin that's messed up. It isn't like it's your soul or something."

She sighed with exasperation, unable to find the words she wanted. "Anyway, I decided I wasn't being fair to you. You hadn't done anything to me, after all. There wasn't any reason for me to have that reaction. I was just going by your appearance, not what kind of person you really are."

He studied her face. "Oh?" he said. "What kind of person am I?"

She shrugged. "I don't know," she said. "I guess that's what I'm here to find out."

For a moment they stood staring at each other. Then Susan cleared her throat.

"Can I, uh, put this down somewhere?" she asked, giving him an uncertain smile and raising the casserole and eating implements.

He seemed to notice the crock of hot food for the first time. Shaking himself back to attention he stepped away from the door. "Sure," he said. "God, I'm so sorry—it's been so long since I entertained guests, I'm afraid I forgot my manners. Put it down on the counter in the kitchenette."

She did as he suggested. The tiny kitchen was neat. The counter had an electric coffee maker at one end and a bowl and a mug in a dish drainer above the sink. A clean steel teaspoon like those sold in supermarkets sat in a slotted plastic container in the drainer's corner. No food visible anywhere in the room but a 750-milliliter whisky bottle sat next to the drainer. An uncapped twin already half empty next to it.

The big man spotted her looking at the bottles. He seemed as embarrassed to be caught drinking so early in the day as he was by his scars. "That sure smells good," he said, nodding toward the casserole. "What did you say it was again?"

"Macaroni and cheese," Susan said, depositing the dinnerware on the bare table and setting the steaming container of pasta and sauce next to it. "Sorry it's not something better, but I work as a nurse and go to school a couple nights a week, so

I didn't have a lot of time to get it together."

"What's the occasion?" he asked.

"I dunno," she said, looking him directly in the eye. "We're neighbors, that's all. I thought it might be sort of neighborly to get to know each other, just in case there was some sort of emergency or something. At least that way we would have each other's names."

She put out her hand. "So, just to take it from the top, I'm Susan Carnes," she said. "And you are...?"

He stared at her hand for a second then slowly took it in his own. "My name is Alan Baldocchi."

She was surprised that despite the waxy, wet look of the scar tissue, it felt dry. They shook in silence, and she giggled involuntarily.

"We certainly managed to turn that into a solemn occasion," she said. "You'd think I just borrowed a bunch of money from you."

His face contorted strangely. "Sorry," he said. "That's supposed to be a smile. I'm not so good at it anymore, what with all this." He waved the stumpy remains of his free hand in a circle around his face to indicate the scar tissue. "The scarring is too stiff for normal expression, I'm afraid. When I smile, it looks more like I just had a tooth pulled."

Susan noticed she was still holding his hand. She was surprised to find she didn't really feel like letting it go. For some reason, she felt comfortable with him, despite his size and hideous scars. Somehow she knew he would never harm her.

She looked into his eyes and saw both mental and physical pain there. Her first impression of him could not have been more wrong—he was a gentle soul trapped in a disfigured body. There was nothing creepy about him.

She realized he had said something while she was lost in thought.

"I'm sorry," she said. "What was that again?"

"Have you eaten yet?" he asked.

She smiled. "No, actually—I haven't. That's why I brought two forks and two plates. Do you mind if I join you?"

He grimaced his peculiar version of a smile again. "Not at all," he said. "I'd enjoy the company."

***

"Check this out," Marcel said to Sonny Jackson as they sat on the Claymore's stoop.

He held open his Oakland Raider jacket and pulled a dark blue semiautomatic pistol out of his waistband far enough so Sonny could get a good look at it. It was an old Army model .45-caliber, the primary sidearm for U.S. military personnel until the mid-1980s.

"Jesus, man!" Sonny said, his eyes bright with excitement. "Where'd you get it?"

Marcel grinned as he tucked it back into his

coat and pulled up the zipper. To Marcel the gun felt big enough to fill the trunk of a car but it was barely visible stuffed down inside his jacket.

"Lonnie Tucker," he said. "He needed a half pound of Tina but didn't have the bread to pay for it. I asked him what he had for trade and he said the gun. Two full magazines, too."

Sonny wrinkled his brow. "I thought you wanted two grand for a pound of crank. That old gun is all scratched up and dinged. A grand is an awful lot of money for a used gun, man. Pinkie Sanders got his Glock for only two hundred."

"The beaners only charge me about $500 for that meth and I step on it myself to move on the street. If I pump it up to two grand a pound, I can sell it at cost, too. Besides, Pinkie's Glock is hotter than a habañero. Alonzo Booker was the last one that used that gun and he shot that A-rab with it when he stuck up the liquor store in Otisville."

"Yeah, but that A-rab din't die, Marcel," Sonny said. "I heard he was back behind the counter the next day."

"Mox nix," Marcel said with a shrug. "The feds are looking for that gun now. Bureau of Alcohol Tobacco and Firearms. Pinkie gets caught with it, he's going to end up wearing an orange jumpsuit. And when the feds grab you, you do the whole jolt, no parole. It's not like a state beef."

"No shit?" Sonny said. That's why he liked

hanging out with Marcel: the guy was smart. All the other guys on the stoop ran their mouths, but Marcel knew what he was talking about.

Marcel patted the gun under his jacket and grinned. "I shoot some A-rab with this piece, that motherfucker's dead, bro. Pinkie's Glock is a nine mill. This here's a forty-five: it's powerful enough to knock a man down with one shot."

"So where'd Lonnie get it?" Sonny asked.

Marcel shrugged. "He and Art Castiglia broke into some rich fucker's house over on Hillside. They took off a whole potful of jewelry from the guy's old lady: gold, gems, that silvery stuff that costs as much as gold. They found the gun downstairs in a desk drawer and Lonnie held onto it, figuring it would be worth something to him sooner or later."

"So, what you planning to do with it?" Sonny asked.

Marcel pulled out the pistol and racked the slide like he'd seen somebody do in a movie once. He pointed it into the street and squinted down the barrel.

"Maybe I'll pull it on that cunt of a nurse upstairs, the white bitch who's so fucking snooty. I been sniffing around her for a couple months now and she won't give me the time of day. I bet I'd get a taste of her sugar if I put this under her chin."

Sonny's expression changed. He swallowed loudly and looked nervous.

"What?" Marcel said.

"You didn't hear, then?" Sonny said.

"Hear what?"

"That soldier guy," Sonny said. "Apparently him and that nurse got something going on. She took dinner up to his apartment the other night. They ate together."

Marcel's eyes narrowed with anger. "She gives me the brush but has dinner with that ugly motherfucker?" His voice squeaked with anger. "That skank makes Bitsy look like a fucking nun and everybody in the district knows what a slut Bits is."

He looked at the pistol in his hand, grinding his teeth with rage. "I'd like to shove this fucking gun up her twat and give her a lead douche," he said, hefting the .45 in his hand. "I'll figure something out, don't worry about it," he growled, jamming the pistol back into his waistband.

***

Baldocchi rarely slept more than a couple hours before the dream about hitting the IED woke him up.

It always started out the same: with him and the commander inspecting the vehicle while the rest of the squad—the dismounts—slogged out to the Bradley M2A2 with their gear slung over their shoulders, climbed into the big tin can and hunkered down for patrol.

Baldocchi was the gunner, sitting up with the 25 millimeter chain gun on the right side of the turret, right next to the commander.

The turret position gave him a bit more room than being packed in the space below, but he was too big for the damned thing, and ended up with a backache every time they ran a mission. He preferred riding with the hatch open, standing up, though it made him a target for the insurgents his unit was supposed to be fighting.

The Commander, Castlewood, preferred to keep the top down, using his periscope array to navigate the vehicle and calling down to the driver.

The driver, a new guy named Olson, was laid back on the left side forward, using scopes to see where he was going and look for obstructions. He was the greenhorn: he'd been through the TRADOC school and was rated on the M2A2, but the Army'd had him driving Humvees up until the last week when the Bradley's regular driver, Kilmer, rotated back to the states. He was still having trouble orienting himself by looking through the scopes.

Both Castlewood and Olson had hatches they could open, but they preferred looking through the tubes because they were nervous about exposure to insurgents on patrol. Baldocchi closed his when they entered an area where they were likely to come under fire, but he kept the top up as much as possible so he could stretch and avoid the back pain he got from crouching inside the turret.

It was a clumsy set up, but there wasn't anything that could be done about it: it was just the way the M2A2 was designed.

On the day the Bradley burned, Baldocchi climbed into his rig, strapped up and put on the VIS headset that let him communicate with the rest of the crew. When the vehicle was loaded, he gave Castlewood the all clear and they pulled out of the base camp, followed by a hard-target Humvee with another squad of infantry aboard.

They had completed about half of their 150-mile patrol circuit in Nuristan Province and had hit the fork in the road at a pivot point they dubbed "Utah." To Baldocchi, still riding high in the turret, the split didn't look right for some reason. There was a pile of rubble on the roadway that looked suspicious. He used his headset to let Castlewood know about it.

"There's shit in the road up ahead," he said. "Maybe we should stop and get out to take a look."

"Where?" Castlewood said. "I don't see anything."

Castlewood didn't like getting out of the M2. During his first tour of Afghanistan, he had been in a convoy that came under attack and the infantry unit he was transporting took heavy casualties. Two Humvees were destroyed by enemy fire, and the damage that RPGs had done to the vehicles made him leery of stepping outside an armored transport.

Baldocchi, forgetting that he was the only one who could see his gesture, pointed to the left fork of the road.

"It's over there," he said.

Olson's voice came across the intercom. "Where? I got nothing in my scopes."

"It's on the left," he said anxiously as the Bradley continued to shoot along at close to twenty miles per hour.

"Go to your left," Castlewood told Olson, misunderstanding Baldocchi.

"OK, left," Olson responded. "Right, I got it."

"No, turn to the right," Baldocchi said as the Bradley neared the pile.

"Jesus, Sarge, make up your mind, would you?" Castlewood said.

The rubble was directly in front of the Bradley. The armored vehicle would pass over it in a second or two.

"Take the right," Baldocchi said with a panicky edge to his voice. "The right. The right.

Take the right fork; there's something wrong with the road on the left hand side!"

"Roger that," Olson said, swerving at the last moment as the Bradley began to pass over the rubble. But he turned too late and the left hand side of the Bradley passed directly over the pile.

Baldocchi couldn't remember anything about the first explosion. It must have been a sonofabitch, though, because it lifted the 28-ton vehicle in the air before dumping it on its right hand side 20 feet away. If the Bradley had tipped a little further over, Baldocchi's scars wouldn't matter because the vehicle would have rolled over him, crushing his upper body between its turret and hatch cover as it did.

Whatever had been in the IED was powerful enough to split the Bradley's hull in a couple of the weak places on its underside. He hung in his web safety belts, only semi-conscious, and could smell the greasy odor of diesel fuel as it gurgled out into the passenger compartment below.

He was vaguely aware of a smoky scent, too, and the sickening sweetness of cooking flesh. The explosion had left him dazed with his head spinning, but in the back of his mind he realized that something inside the Bradley was on fire.

He struggled to unfasten the nylon webbing of his safety harness but his hands didn't seem to want to grip. Instead, he pawed ineffectively at the material, swearing at its resistance until it occurred to him that his fingers might be broken.

He might not have been able to remember the first blast, but the second one was burned vividly into his memory. That was the one that happened inside the hull of the Bradley when sufficient diesel fuel leaked out to reach the vehicle's short-circuiting electronics.

It caused an eruption of burning diesel that coated his body from just above his knees to the inside of his helmet. The fuel exploded, making his inability to get out of his safety harness moot: the force of the blast simply threw him out of the vehicle, breaking both his shoulders and shredding the nylon straps that confined him. He landed about two and a half meters from the burning vehicle, screaming with agony as the flames swallowed him. Fortunately a blast of carbon dioxide gas quickly extinguished the fire and soothed him as the first of the G.I.s from the Humvee reached him with an extinguisher.

His last words to Olson echoed in his head as he slowly came out of his fitful sleep. *Take the right,* Baldocchi had said with a panicky edge to his voice. *The right. The right. Take the right fork; there's something wrong with the road on the left hand side!*

Why won't anyone listen to me?

***

Jerking awake in the darkness, Baldocchi lay in

his bed and listened to the dry rasp of his lungs as he struggled to catch his breath. It was the fourth time in the last six days he had lived through the nightmare.

When he first woke up in the surgical unit outside Kabul, he recalled the entire incident from beginning to end every single time he closed his eyes. Four nights out of six was real progress, he thought.

Maybe by the time he was 85, he would be dreaming about the explosion and fire only a couple of times a month.

***

"Did you win the lottery or something?" Dr. Smith said as he washed his hands in the examining room, sneaking a glance at Baldocchi's face in the little mirror above the sink.

Baldocchi finished buttoning his shirt before responding.

"Not unless you can win without buying a ticket," he said. "Why do you ask?"

Smith folded his arms on his chest. "For one thing, you haven't bitched once about how badly you feel since you walked into the office," he said. "You took your clothes off without complaining and you've been here twenty minutes but haven't told me you would probably be better off dead in Afghanistan than alive in the United States. Your attitude seems to be improving. Did you join a book club or something?"

Baldocchi pulled his trench coat around him and picked up his cap. "I guess I do feel a bit less depressed," he said. "I've made a friend."

Smith grinned. "I should have guessed. Who is he?"

"It's a she, not a he," Baldocchi said. "She lives in my apartment house."

"Good for you!" Smith said. "What does she do for a living?"

Baldocchi wasn't sure how to answer. "I don't know, to be honest," he said after a thoughtful pause. "I mean, she told me she's a nurse and works at a hospital like this one—St. Bart's, over on 31st and Jay. But I don't know her area of specialization."

The fact is that he hadn't really had an opportunity to find out while they shared the macaroni and cheese a couple of nights earlier. She had asked most of the questions during the meal and he did the answering. She seemed genuinely interested in where he came from, where he had gone to school, how he'd come to be in the Army, serving in Afghanistan. When he finished answering one of her questions, she would ask him another. She seemed nervous about filling any lapses. And despite her obvious curiosity she hadn't asked him how he'd been injured.

"So is this a serious relationship?" Smith asked.

Baldocchi shrugged. "It's a friendship," he said. "Nothing more. But at this point, even a routine friendship is serious to me. The only friends I had were in the Bradley when that IED went off and they're all dead. I've been a little reluctant to get too close to anybody since."

"Understandable," Smith said. "Still, having somebody else to think about has to be good for you. Maybe it will get you out of this funk you've been in. It might even give you a reason to stop drinking so much."

Baldocchi's smile looked more like a rictus than a grin. Regardless, he turned it loose on Smith now.

"Let's take it one step at a time," he told the doctor. "I'd like to see how our friendship shapes up before I start rearranging the rest of my life around it. I'll stop drinking when I decide I don't need something to fall back on. I haven't reached that point yet. I'm nowhere near it."

***

Oscar One-Eye had only been old enough to legally enter Gloria's Tavern for the last eight months, though he'd been hanging out at the place since his junior year at Benjamin Harrison high.

Marcel's entire posse frequented the joint, even though the owner, Gloria DeSanto, had started carding and 86ing them and their friends in an effort to discourage them from making it their headquarters. The Eastland Avenue Bloods a block away were the local top dogs and Gloria didn't want her joint to get the rep of favoring one group of 'bangers over the other. When a gang took over a bar, locals avoided it and their rivals tagged hell out of it in an effort to gain a foothold in the territory.

Oscar was too broke for anything but bottled beer and he had to make that last, so he had learned how to spend more than an hour using his fingernails to scrape the label off a bottle of Pabst in one complete piece. His pastime gave him lots of time to watch the other customers. Occasionally one who had money in his pocket would get up and stagger home. When he did, Oscar would follow him and lighten his wallet when he reached a spot that was dark enough.

Tonight looked like it was going to be a big night, Oscar thought.

The ex-soldier Sonny Jackson had dubbed "Freddie Krueger," was at the bar, knocking back Jim Beam Rye like he had stock in the company. The big man had already chased four shots with Miller draft, and he was scraping his change together and counting out a number of bills to leave on the counter as a tip.

Oscar got up, leaving his empty on the corner

table where he'd been sitting. He walked out of Gloria's, crossed the street, stood in the dry cleaner's doorway so he could clock the big man when he left.

***

"You okay, mister?" Gloria said as Baldocchi stood up, stumbled a half step backward and drew himself up.

The big man belched involuntarily. "'Scuse me," he said. "I think I may have had a little too much to drunk."

He sounded pretty wasted. He had a scarf swathed around the lower half of his face and a cap pulled down so all she could see were his bloodshot eyes.

He hiccuped and spread his tip money out on the bar top. "'Sfor you, ma'am," he slurred. "Thanks very much."

"You want me to call you a cab, mister?"

The big man waved a hand dismissively. "Not necessary," he said, hiccuping. "I live up the street in the Claymore. I can walk it myself. The fresh air will clear my head."

He gave her a salute, swung in a half circle and lurched to the doorway, leaving DeSanto shaking her head behind the bar.

***

Oscar was sure that the big man was shitfaced as soon as he walked through the bar's door, stepped off the curb and nearly fell into the street. G.I. Joe was heading for the Claymore, but he was using a lot more steps than were necessary to cover the distance.

The stoop boy wrapped his hand around the black jack stuffed in his coat pocket. The feel of the hard, smooth surface pumped up his nerve.

There was an alley in the middle of the next block that would be as good a spot as any to make his move: somebody had chucked a rock through the lone street lamp and the only doorway in the alley was dark.

***

Baldocchi stepped gingerly, his head fogged by whisky and beer. He had both hands jammed in the pockets of his olive drab trench coat and hummed a snatch of *Round Midnight* tunelessly as he plunged forward, repeating the passage over and over because it was the only part of the song he could remember.

He was drunk, but not so drunk he hadn't spotted the kid from the Claymore's front stoop back in Gloria's, eyeballing him from the corner table. Didn't require much sobriety to know the kid was sizing him up for a mugging. When he spotted the darkened alley a half block ahead, instincts he had honed in combat during one and a half Army tours told him that was where the kid would try to take him. Adrenaline pumped into his bloodstream, clearing his head and setting his nerves on edge exactly as it had on patrol in Afghanistan.

Baldocchi stopped for a moment to lean against a street lamp. He didn't really need to make the stop, but he wanted the kid who was dogging his steps to think he did. He pushed away, taking two steps sideways toward the alley—he figured if he was off-balance and already seemed to be aimed in that direction, the kid would make his move.

He was right.

Oscar One-eye took three steps to close the distance and slammed into Baldocchi's left shoulder from behind, shoving him into the darkness. The stoop boy pulled the blackjack out of his pocket and swung it back, setting himself up to fracture the big man's skull.

He never had the chance.

Back in the bar, Baldocchi had slipped a molded glass ashtray into his jacket pocket as soon as Gloria wiped it and put it down in front of him. One-eye spotted the ashtray an instant before Baldocchi slammed its corner into his temple.

The thick glass shattered from the impact with the 'banger's skull, fracturing his cranium and rolling his eyes up like a pair of window shades. The force of the blow swept Oscar to the ground. He reached out with his right arm in an effort to break the fall. His humerus snapped as it contacted the ground, punching the ragged end of the bone through Oscar's biceps.

Baldocchi stood over the unconscious mugger, panting. The rush from the brief struggle had flushed the rest of the alcohol from his system. Something wet dripped onto his shoe and he raised his hand to see where it had come from. A torrent of blood ran down his arm, soaking his long-sleeved shirt and flooding the inside of his trench coat's sleeve.

He opened the burned stumps of his fingers. What was left of the ashtray clattered to the ground in a spray of red.

***

After the cops took his statement, two paramedics drove Baldocchi to St. Bart's for stitches to close the rips in his hand. A second ambulance had already rushed Oscar One-eye to the county trauma center; Baldocchi overheard one of the cops say the gangbanger needed emergency surgery because the broken bone in his arm had opened an artery and he was going into shock.

***

There were 18 other people waiting to be seen when Baldocchi arrived at St. Bart's emergency room. The paramedics swaddled his stumpy hand in gauze but the fabric was immediately dyed red by blood seeping from his wounds. He sat in silence, his head down, still dazed by the fight with Oscar One-eye.

"What are you doing here?"

He looked up. It was Susan Carnes, dressed in greens with a stethoscope hanging around her neck, its business end in her breast pocket.

The light from the hospital's fluorescent fixtures gave everything and everybody in the hallway a flat, washed-out look, but it also let Baldocchi get his first clear look at the nurse. Even in the shapeless medical uniform and a hairnet she was remarkably attractive.

"I could ask you the same question," he said. "I thought you worked days at the hospital."

To his surprise, she slid onto the seat next to him on the bench. There was plenty of room because the people on either side of Baldocchi had moved as far as they could from the scarred man, almost as if they feared his disfigurement had been caused by some highly infectious disease rather than a Taliban bomb.

"Just getting off shift," she said. "I swapped with another nurse who needed the evening off. My question still stands, though."

She gently lifted his arm with the bandaged hand. "Cut yourself shaving?"

He shrugged and made the face that substituted for a smile. "I stopped at the bar,

Gloria's, for a few drinks," he said. "One of those gang kids that hang out on the apartment steps was there. He must have thought I looked like I'd be easy to rob."

She frowned. "Did you file a complaint against him?" she asked.

"I didn't have to. They took him to the county hospital's ICU unit." He made the face again, though it clearly hurt. "His head got in the way of a big glass ashtray. They told me I fractured his skull."

"This was in Gloria's?" she asked, shocked at his seemingly casual attitude about what to her sounded like a grotesque act of violence.

He shook his head. "Outside. He tried to steer me into an alley but I was ready for him." He raised his bandaged hand. "I was holding the ashtray like this. He tried to club me with a blackjack, so I hit him. The sharp pieces of glass cut my hand."

She looked at him the way she had in his apartment—directly, without blinking. "You knew he was going to try it." She shook her head with disbelief. "You deliberately took him on. It almost sounds like you were trying to get attacked."

"Let's say I had a hunch it would happen," he said. "A shrink would probably say I have a death wish or something."

She sneered. "So would I." She got up and

gave his arm a tug. "Come with me. You'll be sitting here in the passageway all night, otherwise."

She led him into a room next to the receptionist and told him to sit down on a gurney pushed up against the wall.

"Take off your hat and shirt," she said, crossing her arms under her small breasts.

"Why?" he said. "I only hurt my hand."

"Just do it," she said, sticking a thermometer under his tongue. Baldocchi did as she told him. He thought she sounded more like a doctor than most doctors do.

She used a stethoscope to listen to his heart and lungs, took his pulse and checked his blood pressure with the Judas cuff before she turned her attention to his cuts. It took her a few minutes to unwind the gauze and examine his hand. Three wounds—two in the palm and a shorter one in the web between his thumb and fingers.

"You were lucky," she said as she used a forceps to pick little bits of glass out of the openings and swabbed the cuts with antiseptic. "This one on your thumb: if it had been a little deeper, it would have severed the tendon. You'd have needed surgery."

"People keep telling me how lucky I am," he said. "Maybe I should buy some lottery tickets or enter that Publisher's Clearing House sweepstakes. I'd clean up."

She gave him an exasperated look. "You're one of the most sarcastic people I've ever met."

He grunted a sort of laugh. "I just happen to think life's a bitch, that's all."

"It's a hell of a lot better than the alternative," she said, using butterfly sutures to close his cuts.

"Not with these," he said, using one of his stumpy hands to wave at the extensive scar tissue that covered his upper body from the crown of his head to his belt line. "I feel like Frankenstein's monster and that's how most people treat me."

She applied another butterfly closure. "How did you get those?" she asked. "I wanted to ask you the other night when we had dinner together, but I couldn't think of a good way to raise the subject."

"It was random, really," he said, "just one of those damned things that happen to people during wars. My unit ran into a homemade bomb alongside the road in Afghanistan."

He glanced at her to see how she reacted and was surprised to see she was still looking directly at him. He'd expected she would turn her eyes away from his waxy skin; even his doctor did.

"Were you on foot?" she asked.

He shook his head. "I was in an armored personnel carrier. Unfortunately, most of the armor was stuff we tacked on when we got to Kabul. It was typical Army junk—not really set up for the job it was supposed to do. They say we always prepare for the last war we fought. In this case, it's true. Our vehicle was supposed to be combat ready, but it was really only fit for little runs around the base in the U.S."

"You were—inside it, then?"

He nodded. "Sort of. I was the gunner, in a little turret on top. The explosion blew me out of the thing and broke both my shoulders."

"What happened to the rest of your unit?"

"All killed," he replied. "I was the only one who got out alive—and you can see what kind of shape I'm in. The other guys burned to a crisp."

She shook her head, imagining what it must have been like. "I still don't understand how the scarring happened."

"The fuel in the Bradley's tank exploded from the bomb. The blast shot me out the top, but sprayed me with burning diesel fuel. There were some English guys from another unit up ahead of us who missed the bomb and a police jeep going by the other direction when it went off—Afghans, not American G.I.s. The cops and the Brits used fire extinguishers to smother the fire."

"Wow!" she said. "It must have been awful!"

"I still have dreams about it They're the kind of dreams you're happy to wake up from."

"Well," she said, smiling at him. "If the police hadn't put out the flames, you never would have met me. And if you'd been killed by that little bastard tonight, you wouldn't be sitting here with me holding your hand like this."

He realized that she hadn't released it when she finished putting the sutures on. Her hands were soft and warm and she smiled. Her gentle way of showing him that, though she was kidding, she wasn't really kidding.

"One of the ER surgeons would have kept you waiting another hour or so before sewing you up and sending you a bill," she said. "But those wounds are really superficial and should heal fine by themselves so long as you keep them dry for the next 24 hours and put fresh Band-Aids on them when these come loose. Have you had a tetanus vaccination in the last couple of years?"

He nodded. "Yeah—when I got myself fried in Afghanistan the explosion peppered me with shrapnel. They dug out 124 pieces of it at the field hospital and another 43 when I got back stateside."

His tone was defiant. He was trying to shock her, but it didn't work.

"You shouldn't need any other treatment, then," she said matter-of-factly, as if most of her patients had been blown up by bombs.

She looked him straight in the eye the way she had when she brought the macaroni and cheese over. It was different from her reaction on the staircase the first time they'd met; then she'd seemed to find him frightening, disgusting. Now when she stared at him it was like she didn't really notice his waxy, gooey-looking skin; it was more as if she couldn't understand why he had such a bad attitude.

"Look. I understand the bomb left you a physical mess, but it seems to me you spend an awful lot of your time dwelling on it." She held his injured hand gently in both of hers. "You've got it tough, no doubt about it. I can see how much you've suffered every time I look at those scars.

"But you're not the only person in the world who's had bad luck. You can still walk, you can hear and you can see. Why don't you try using your eyes to look on the positive side for a change? The world is drowning in shit, but manure grows roses, too. If I were you, I'd ignore the crap and spend more time concentrating on the flowers."

Without thinking she leaned forward and planted a soft kiss in the middle of his forehead. If someone had asked her why, she wouldn't have been able to explain.

Baldocchi hadn't been kissed by a woman since he left the U.S. for his second tour in Afghanistan. He touched the spot where her lips had pressed. He could feel the blood rush to his head and his mouth went as dry as it did when he was on recon outside Kandahar in the middle of the summer.

Most people tippy-toed around instead of saying what was on their minds; it was refreshing to meet somebody as blunt as he was for a change.

"How are you getting home?" she asked him.

"I have no idea," he said. "Bus, I guess. I hadn't given it any thought."

She smiled. "Let's share a cab. I'm officially finished with my shift. I was leaving when I saw you in the ER. You take the bus, you'll be waiting all night."

She cocked her head to one side and took a long look at the glassy skin that covered his torso. "It's not as bad as you think, you know?" she said, gazing into his eyes again.

"What isn't?"

She gestured loosely at his chest. "Your disfigurement. You aren't going to win any beauty contests, but it isn't your scarred skin that makes people look away from you."

"It's not?" he asked.

She shook her head. "It's the toxic attitude you're carrying around inside it."

He stood and grabbed his shirt with the grimace that substituted for a smile. "Whatever," he said. "But if we're going to leave through the ER waiting room, I better put some clothes on. I wouldn't want anybody fainting because of my bad attitude."

***

When Sonny and Luis found Marcel, the gang leader had Bitsy on a table in the side hallway of the Carleton with her underpants down and her legs up alongside his ears. He seemed pissed to have been caught having sex with the stoop girl. She didn't look any happier to have him banging her in front of two of his posse.

Sonny watched her primp her pink hair and plant a kiss on Marcel's forehead before she hustled off with a brusque "Later, babe!" Luis had to look away to make sure the gang leader didn't see him grin.

Marcel didn't take the news about Oscar One-eye well at all.

"He's where?" he asked Sonny, his voice climbing a half octave.

"The county hospital, boss," Sonny said. "His mamma said he's in a coma. The cops came by to fill her in. They said he tried to hijack a guy who was leaving Gloria's and the guy half knocked his brains out."

Marcel struggled to understand. How could Oscar end up underestimating a mark that badly? He must have strong-armed a dozen drunks leaving the place in the last couple of years. He always took them from behind and used a sap to knock them out. No way that a mugging like that could go sour. No way at all.

"Jesus Christ," Marcel said. "That's fucking pathetic. Oscar must have been loaded or something. This is going to take some serious payback, man. We're the 14th Avenue Crips. We can't let some fucking square beat down one of our own. Who was the guy he tried to rob?"

Sonny and Luis Cardeña exchanged glances. It never paid to be the one who gave Marcel bad news.

"It was that big guy with the scars." Luis swallowed hard.

Marcel's eyes widened. "You mean G.I. Joe had the balls to crack Oscar's skull?"

Luis and Sonny both nodded hurriedly. Marcel seemed to be madder at the guy with the burns than them. That would probably save both of them an ass-whipping for seeing him skewer Bitsy on the sly.

"So what happened to Freddie Krueger?" Marcel asked. "Did Oscar get a couple of shots in?"

Sonny licked his lips. "Oscar's mom says they had to take scarface to the hospital, too, but to St. Bart's, not county ICU."

"Wait a minute," Marcel said, shutting his eyes, his anger flaring even higher. "You say Oscar's in intensive care but this burned soldier guy isn't?"

Sonny nodded fearfully. "Yeah, Marce. Oscar's mom says that the cops told her the guy cut his hand, is all."

Marcel put his thumbs in his waistband and slid them outward, opening the front of his jacket so you could see the butt of the .45 sticking up.

"That fucking soldier boy wants a war with the 14th Avenue Crips, it's on," he hissed. "We'll get a two-fer: we'll have a little fun with his girlfriend, that skanky nurse, then we'll kill the sonofabitch. Period. End of fucking report. That motherfucker's going down."

***

When the adrenaline faded out of his system, Baldocchi crashed like a speed freak. He struggled out of the cab and up the stairs of the Claymore with Susan tucked under his left arm like a human crutch. The elevator—which was working for once—shuddered when she helped him stumble into it and he had to let her use his key to open the door to his apartment.

He collapsed onto his tiny double bed with a crash that nearly collapsed it and began to snore raggedly as Susan removed his shoes and socks and lifted his feet onto the mattress. She left quietly, wary of waking him.

***

It could have been the booze he'd consumed at Gloria's, the stress of the fight with Oscar One-

Eye, or the release of telling Susan how he'd become such a walking disaster zone, but Baldocchi began unreeling the dream as soon as he passed out.

If only he'd been clearer in his instructions to the Bradley's driver, they might have missed the IED completely.

He would never have been rushed to the hospital. He might still be in Afghanistan.

"Jesus, Sarge, make up your mind, would you?" Castlewood had said.

He still couldn't, after all this time. Every night before he dropped off to sleep, he still wondered: was he glad he had survived or sorry he was still living?

In his dream the rubble was directly in front of the Bradley, the explosion only seconds away.

Jesus, Sarge, make up your mind, would you?

Take the right, Baldocchi mumbled, still coming out of the dream. *Take the right fork; there's something wrong with the road on the left hand side!*

But this time the dream did not end with the death and destruction that actually occurred. Olson was quicker to acknowledge Baldocchi's order and veered away from the rubble a second or two before the bomb exploded. In his revised nightmare, the blast washed the left side of Baldocchi's face with searing heat, but the pain was nothing like the gusher of liquid fire that had killed the other members of his unit and left him hideously scarred.

For an instant, the Bradley teetered on one track, then collapsed onto its side. Beneath him, inside the APC, Baldocchi could hear the muffled cries of one of his teammates.

Help! Help me!

With a gasp, he woke up.

Help me!

The voice he had heard was not a fantasy. It was real—and it was coming from the room directly below him.

He hoisted himself up and swung his feet into his loafers, his alcoholic dehydration sending a flash of pain ripping through his head that made him gasp with agony.

Covering his face with both hands he listened. Then he heard it again—the sound of a woman in pain.

Staggering to his feet, Baldocchi lurched to the door, held himself up by it for a second while his head swam, then plunged through it and down the stairs.

The cries grew louder as he neared Susan's apartment.

"Susan, are you okay?" he called, hesitating in the hall outside.

His hand closed on the apartment's doorknob and he gave it a turn. As he did, the door swung inward, dragging him off-balance into the room. Something hard and heavy crashed into the back of his head, driving him down and forward into a small coffee table that buckled and splintered under his weight.

He rolled over and saw one of the stoop boys standing over him, swinging a baseball bat in a hard arc at his forehead. Baldocchi managed to move just as the aluminum cylinder buried itself in the wreckage of the table.

He recognized the youth as the one called Sonny and kicked hard with his right foot as the kid swung the bat again. Sonny took the kick in the stomach, landing next to the door with an impact that made the entire building shudder.

Baldocchi was up surprisingly fast. Sonny plunged forward with a snarl and Alan punched him in the middle of his face, sending his head back into the wall with a second crash even louder than the first.

His eyes wide and staring, Sonny slid down, his head leaving a dark streak of blood on the wallpaper next to the door frame, a two-inch deep crater where Alan's punch had pushed the back of the kid's skull through the plaster.

Sonny slowly toppled to his right, his open mouth dripping blood onto the oak planks of the floor.

Baldocchi turned to see the gangbanger called

Marcel holding Susan down on her table, her uniform skirt pushed up over her breasts. Her panties were gone, apparently ripped off by the youth when he attacked her. There was a small puddle of fluid on the tabletop.

The gang leader looked straight at Baldocchi. His eyes were like those of an animal, his pupils dilated to the size of dimes.

Marcel had one of his hands over Susan's mouth to muffle her cries. The other held a Buck knife poised for a strike to her throat. The gang member seemed to be frozen in place, staring at Alan with disbelief as he tried to figure out how he had managed to shrug off a clubbing that should have cracked his skull, then take out one of his strongest, fastest gang members with little effort.

Baldocchi grabbed Marcel by the lapels of his Oakland Raider's jacket and yanked him off the nurse so hard that the youth was suspended in midair for a fraction of a second. As he spun him halfway around, he saw Marcel's trousers were unzipped and his dick—long, hard and twisted slightly to the left—protruded from his open fly. Marcel grabbed one of Baldocchi's wrists with both hands and his knife clattered on the bare tile floor.

Overcome with fury, Baldocchi pulled back his right hand and drove his fist into the youth's face, crushing his nose with a pulpy crunching sound. He let go of the gang member as he threw the punch and the stoop boy slammed against the base of the wall in an awkward heap.

"Are you all right?" Alan asked Susan hoarsely as he helped her sit up on the table and held one of her hands in both of his.

She stared at him stupidly, shock clouding her face. Her eyes focused on something behind him. They widened as she screamed.

Baldocchi turned halfway around and the scene registered on his brain like a still photograph: Marcel, halfway to his feet, had pulled an old Army pistol. He managed to aim the gun at Baldocchi's chest and pull the trigger, punching a half-inch hole in the scarred man's front and a much wider one in his back.

The shot sounded like a bomb in the nurse's tiny apartment. The ear-ringing explosion and the recoil of the pistol startled Marcel so much that he dropped the gun on the floor.

Baldocchi made an animal sound in his throat and grabbed the stoop boy with his stubby hands. He swung Marcel wildly, his burned fingers clasped tightly around the youth's neck, half dragging him across the room. The gang member's eyes protruded from their sockets. A gurgling hiss escaped from his mouth like the wail of a small, frightened animal.

Then Baldocchi hurled him through the window hard enough to shatter it and splinter its sill.

Marcel was airborne before he had a chance to scream, taking the pane and most of the glass with him all the way to the concrete sidewalk three stories below. He might have survived the plunge if he hadn't landed head first on the pavement with enough force to pulverize his skull and everything inside it.

Baldocchi turned back to Susan, air whistling slightly through the gore-filled bullet hole in his chest as it sucked blood into his lungs with a gurgle. He stepped forward clumsily like a man trying to wade a creek. Then he toppled to the floor.

Susan sank to her knees, cradling his head and comforting him in a whisper as she struggled to close his chest wound with the palm of her hand.

"Don't move," she murmured. "I won't be able to stop the bleeding if you don't hold still. Help'll be here soon, Alan. Just hold on. Everything will be fine."

He covered her hand with his and looked up into her face. "Not this time," he gasped. "You get one do over in this world. Mine was in Afghanistan."

Tears welled in her eyes. "Don't say that," she whispered. "You'll be fine."

But she knew it wasn't true. She could feel his life pumping out under her fingers. There was no way to stop it.

He squeezed her hand. "I want you to do something for me," he rasped. "My doctor at the V.A. is Clinton Smith. Dr. Clinton Smith, internal medicine—can you remember that?"

She nodded and gave him what she hoped was a brave smile.

"Dr. Clinton Smith," she said. "I'll remember."

"I want you to find him, okay?" He gave her hand a hard squeeze then let it slip out of his. "Tell him I found out why God saved me. He'll understand what it means. Can you do that?"

"I promise, Alan," she said.

Baldocchi closed his eyes. His face contorted for the last time and then he was still.

Susan made a small sound in the back of her throat and her tears came freely.

Anyone else would have seen the final twist of his face as the grimace of a man in extreme pain. She knew better.

She could tell Alan Baldocchi had given her his final smile.

About the Author

William E. Wallace has been a cook, dishwasher, journalism professor, private investigator and military intelligence specialist. He received his bachelor's in political science at U.C. Berkeley and for 26 years he was an award-winning investigative reporter for the San Francisco Chronicle. Since taking early retirement in 2006 he has written two detective novels, *The Jade Bone Jar* and *The Judas Hunter*; a novella, *I Wait to Die*; a western novel, *Tamer*; and a collection of horror and fantasy stories, *Little Nightmares*.

His stories have been published in *Flash Fiction Offensive*, *Spinetingler*, *All Due Respect*, *Crime Factory*, *Dark Corners Pulp* and *Shotgun Honey*.

He lives with his wife and son in Berkeley, California.

The following is an excerpt from Alec Cizak's short story collection, Crooked Roads. *For more information on this and other crime fiction titles, check out allduerespectbooks.com.*

THE SPACE BETWEEN

She wears a nametag—Susan. You want her to be more. To see the gray smudges on the bottom of your pants legs, to put a hand on your shoulder and say, "That snow bank sure *seemed* solid." She should notice the gash across your left, index knuckle. Wince at how the wound has turned yellow and brown. "Sometimes we forget to aim the knife away from our bodies," she should say. Beyond that, she should offer empathy over the alimony you can't pay, the money you owe the IRS, the foreclosure. "An apartment might be more manageable, don't you think?" The angle her head rests on her shoulders, the light bouncing off her eyes, the smile she greeted you with when the bell over the front door went 'ding,' these things dissolve layers of hatred gathering mold since your wife insinuated you're a "mama's boy." They cancel the sneers in college, the snubs from attractive sorority girls, the sign stuck to you back in high school (*Kick Me!*).

Your father's fist, once a ton, now evaporates

with a chuckle from you as Susan drops a cliché on the counter—"Cold enough for you?" You don't hear the formality of the situation. You don't realize this relationship is over the moment you pay and walk out the door.

* * *

The creak of your car door slices into your ears and carves canyons in your bones. Did you think the girl at the Kwik Trip would look at you twice? As you turn the ignition and wait for the heater to fire up, watching the fog of your breath splatter against the windshield and shrink, over and over again, you listen to the voice of reason on the radio (*"This country ain't what it used to be?"*) and remember how you will spend the night in a motel with nothing but a television, mini bottles of shampoo, small towels, and a Gideon's Bible that can do nothing to correct mistakes you've made your entire life. Mistakes other people tricked you into making—

Your mother, dressing you in clothes from Second Time Around.

Your father, refusing to look at you after you said you had no interest in baseball.

Junior high girlfriends, lovers, and the wife, calling you one form of inadequate or another.

Would Susan be any different? She doesn't care about you, chump. Look at her now—can't you hear the smacking of her bubblegum? She's in uniform, on the clock, and yet she has her cellphone pasted to her ear. Remember the way she spoke to you, thinking you wouldn't catch the disregard her cliché revealed?

The car's warm.

There's a tire iron in the trunk.

Haven't you reached that point where you could just *drive*?

Made in the USA
Middletown, DE
09 August 2015